"*BEFORE you fell in love with him,*" asked Lady Cresswell, "*did it ever occur to you that he had always had whatever he desired without any effort or hardship on his part?*"

*Pippa opened her mouth to protest—and stopped.*

"*I am not suggesting,*" *Lady Cresswell went on,* "*that you should set up a series of flirts, but it will do him no harm to let it be seen that you are perfectly at home in Society and that you need never lack an escort.*"

*And so Lady Cresswell embarked on a campaign to make her daughter-in-law the toast of London, and the object of her son's astonishment.*

Also by Mira Stables:

| | | |
|---|---|---|
| THE BYRAM SUCCESSION | 23558 | $1.50 |
| FRIENDS AND RELATIONS | 50019 | $1.75 |
| HIGH GARTH | 50032 | $1.75 |
| HONEY POT | 23915 | $1.75 |
| MARRIAGE ALLIANCE | 23929 | $1.75 |
| STRANGER WITHIN THE GATES | 23402 | $1.50 |

8999

# NO IMPEDIMENT

## Mira Stables

FAWCETT COVENTRY ● NEW YORK

For Lizz and Jean
who have married sons of mine
and appear to have survived
with admirable fortitude.

NO IMPEDIMENT

THIS BOOK CONTAINS THE COMPLETE TEXT OF THE
ORIGINAL HARDCOVER EDITION.

Published by Fawcett Coventry Books, a unit of CBS Publi-
cations, the Consumer Publishing Division of CBS Inc. by
arrangement with Robert Hale Limited.

ISBN: 0-449-50080-2

Printed in the United States of America

First Fawcett Coventry printing: August 1980

10  9  8  7  6  5  4  3  2  1

# One

Having reached the sanctuary of the small parlour which he had appropriated to himself for the conduct of estate business, his lordship heaved a sigh of relief, pressed an immaculate handkerchief to a heated brow, and sank thankfully into a chair. Since he had come so unexpectedly into his inheritance, this was his first Public Day. It was amusing—and amazing—to recall that in the days of his childhood Public Days had seemed to him delightful events that came all too rarely. In those days he had found the company far more interesting than that which attended his uncle's formal parties. The tenants and townsfolk brought their children, and there was a good deal of pleasure to be had from showing his pony and the gun that Uncle Howard had had especially built for him for his eighth birthday to certain carefully selected cronies. His friends were not particularly interested in the State Apartments, of course, but the Old Tower, with its ruinous spiral staircase and its blood-stained history, was a sure draw. After Public Days he basked for weeks in the popularity of one who is in the position to provide high treats for his friends.

Today had been very different. Not that he had not enjoyed it, in a sense. But it had been hard work. He had felt that he was treading on eggs. Every tenant must be recognised and greeted with exactly that degree of affability to which his age and standing entitled him. The names of promising offspring must trip off his tongue as though he were personally acquainted with them—which he was not. That was the difficulty, of course. He had not been bred to the job. Had never dreamed that some day all this pomp and circumstance, these English acres and their links with history would be all his. To be honest he would not have wished it so. Merland, to him, had been holiday. He had cheerfully accepted all that it offered—and it offered practically everything that a boy could desire—and had never given a thought to the hours of patient toil, the forethought and diplomacy that went into its maintenance. He had been sincerely fond of Uncle Howard though he preferred to steer clear of Aunt Sophronia. And he had been mildly attached to Cousin Edmund, though he had thought him a bit of a milk-sop, even if he *was* a devil to go on the hunting field. Well—now he knew something of the heavy burden that the poor lad had carried. Small wonder that he had seemed timid and tentative in his decisions when the welfare and prosperity of so many people depended upon them. Perhaps his recklessness in the saddle had been his only escape from the cares that crowded in on him—and from his managing Mama. A sad pity that it had been the cause of his premature death. Even sadder that this should have occurred before there had been time for him to marry and beget an heir. He, Quentin, might never have been saddled with a dignity and responsibility for which he had small taste.

It was not even as though he needed the money, he thought ruefully. Between his father and his mother, he was pretty well to pass. And Town life had suited him very nicely. If one wearied of sophisticated pleasures, there was always Merland. In any case, so far as he had learned during his short incumbency, most of Merland's income went straight back into upkeep and improvement. Which was just as it should be, insisted the voice of inborn instinct. He smiled despite himself, and decided that perhaps, after all, there were the makings of a good landlord within him.

If that were so, it might be as well to tidy up some of his Town affairs. If Merland were to prove an exacting mistress, she would leave scant time for others. In any case, his affair with Cherry had been on the wane even before his succession to Merland. A nice girl, Cherry.

She might be an Opera dancer; she might be his mistress; but she was still a nice girl. She had fully understood the difficulty in which his unexpected inheritance had placed him, and had made no fuss. He might visit her occasionally, for old times' sake, but even that was unlikely.

With a sudden access of energy he rose and crossed to the writing desk which held most of his private papers. From a locked drawer he took a substantial roll of bills which he tucked into an inner pocket of his coat. It spoiled the set of that beautiful garment, but that troubled him not at all. Then he must delve into a 'secret' drawer—a secret that a child might have discovered—in that same desk. It yielded a jeweller's case which, opened, revealed a necklace of rubies and diamonds. A pretty trinket, if not of the first stare, but it was what Cherry had fancied. He had thought that money would have been more sensible, but because she had behaved so well she should have her necklace too. And he might as well set about the business right away. The festivities in the grounds and public rooms would go on for some time yet, and unless he chose to rejoin the guests he would be obliged to skulk in his private apartments. If he could withdraw discreetly, he could be well on the road to Town before darkness obliged him to rack up for the night. Then he could visit Cherry next day and have the whole thing neatly tied up.

His conscience pricked him a little over his desertion but he could rely upon Wetherby. Wetherby had been steward for both his uncle and his cousin. He would cover up beautifully for his delinquent employer. So long as no one actually saw him go, they would simply suppose him to be occupied in some other part of the grounds. And by going through the ballroom, which was not open to visitors, it should be possible to cross the terrace to the stables unperceived.

A quarter of an hour later he might have been seen tiptoeing softly across the ballroom floor. This furtive approach, which was quite unnecessary, and dictated entirely by the insistence of that uneasy conscience, presented a faintly ridiculous appearance, especially when one considered that he was the unquestioned owner of all this spacious grandeur. Since he also carried an overnight bag, having decided to dispense with the services of his valet on this brief and delicate mission, it also presented, to the eyes of a child who was standing with her nose pressed against one of the ballroom windows, a convincing picture of a burglar detected in the act of stealing away with the family silver. Miss Lucinda Merchiston, not yet fourteen, entirely forgot the very doubtful propriety of her own presence on that forbidden terrace. Her eyes widened with mingled shock and delight. Here at last was adventure, as she had always dreamed of it. The proper

9

conduct of the heroine was clear. She was even granted time to rehearse the telling phrases with which she would halt the miscreant, for his lordship was obliged to pause for a moment to wrestle with a stubborn window catch.

Miss Merchiston's reading had not, alas, been supervised with that degree of severity generally held to be desirable. As his lordship eventually emerged on to the terrace he was confronted by a determined little creature who laid resolute if slightly grubby hands upon his valise and announced alarmingly, "Hold, villain! Do not think to escape unhindered with your ill-gotten booty."

At this point memory failed her, and she continued in much more natural tones, "Put that bag down at once, or I shall scream and scream until you do."

His lordship obeyed with commendable promptitude. The last thing he wanted was any kind of hullabaloo. But he was a young man of swift perceptions and had already assessed the situation with a fair degree of accuracy. He could see that the child had some grounds for her rash assumption, and though he was justifiably annoyed by this ridiculous interruption in his proceedings, he was also a little amused. Moreover he was one who rated pluck pretty high in the catalogue of virtues, and it had undoubtedly taken some courage for that scrap to challenge a man of his inches, especially if she supposed him to be an out and out villain.

That did not mean, of course, that he was prepared to knuckle under to her impudent demands.

"Scream away, my girl," he invited her affably. "You should be able to make yourself heard as far as the stables. But while I have every confidence in my ability to prove ownership of the contents of my valise, I very much doubt if *you* have permission to be trespassing on what is undoubtedly private property. I don't know what the penalty is for trespass. But when it is aggravated by threatening behaviour I daresay it merits a stiffish jail sentence."

He wished he had not been quite so brutal. The frank, childish face mirrored each successive emotion, from doubt, at the first sound of the pleasant, educated voice, which certainly did not suggest a criminal background, to apprehension and shock. But she *was* a good plucked 'un, and not ready to yield at the first reverse.

"What reason have I to believe you?" she demanded stoutly, though trembling lips and a voice that was not quite steady betrayed her inner qualms.

His heart melted entirely. "Well, you may look for yourself if you wish," he offered, "but since it contains only a change of linen and my shaving gear perhaps it is scarcely worth it. Try the weight. If it was really filled with valuables, it would be very heavy, you know."

The big brown eyes were still suspicious, but

11

at least she did not take advantage of his offer. In fact she let go her fierce clutch on the valise as she said, "Then why were you creeping out of the window like a thief?"

He drew a solemn face. "If you must know, I am escaping. That is why I didn't really want you to scream. If you had, I might have been caught and obliged to go back."

The delight and excitement in her face betrayed more surely than anything else her extreme youth. Plainly it gave her far more satisfaction to cast him for the rôle of gallant hero escaping from his enemies. She changed sides without a moment's hesitation. "Truly? Oh, how fortunate that I *didn't* scream. But perhaps delay is dangerous. Is there some way in which I can help, to make up for having hindered you?"

His lordship actually entertained the notion of suggesting that she should scout ahead of him to see if the way to the stable was clear, but before he could do so the child suddenly exclaimed, "Oh dear! Here comes Pippa. She will be so cross. You won't tell her that I mistook you for a burglar, will you? It will be quite bad enough without that. The thing is that I did so wish to see the ballroom, and Pippa wouldn't let me. She said it was vulgar and encroaching to push oneself in where one was not invited, and I suppose she is perfectly right. Only when we went to sit beside the lake she fell asleep, and I could see the terrace and the windows and I thought, just one little peep and she would never know. I was—I was tempted beyond my strength," she finished grandly.

His lordship, who had now succumbed entirely to the charm of his young acquaintance, assured her that this was perfectly understandable, and studied the approaching figure. Abigail or governess? Presumably the former, since a governess would surely have been 'Miss Pipper'. His eye was critical. An attendant who fell asleep and allowed her young charge to get into scrapes did not suit his notions of propriety. She was walking swiftly enough now, and noting the erect carriage and the vigorous stride his lordship thought that the wench looked too young for so responsible a position. He had not given any thought to the social standing of this chance-met pair, but presumably they were to be numbered among his guests, and now that he looked at the child closely he assessed her appearance as prosperous to say the least. The dainty cap that framed her face was trimmed with fine needlework and tied with silk ribands, while dress, shoes and stockings, though simple as became a schoolgirl, were of fine quality and tastefully chosen.

Nor was he long left in doubt as to the standing of the new arrival. She was a little breathless from the speed she had made, but no abigail ever spoke in that soft, cultured voice. She favoured him with the tiniest of curtseys as she said, "My apologies, sir, if this runaway has been making a nuisance of herself. It is quite *my* fault for allowing her to escape me, so I hope that you will not scold her too severely but will rather address your displeasure to me."

*Much* too young, confirmed his lordship. She seemed actually to be in sympathy with her charge, concerned only to shield her from retribution.

He said politely, "Your pupil has certainly not annoyed me in any way, nor is it within my province to rebuke you for neglecting your duties. But I sincerely hope that you will be able to impress upon her the danger of wandering off alone in strange surroundings."

It was a very mild reproof, but it caused the wench to colour up furiously and moved his former ally to exclaim indignantly, "It wasn't Pippa's fault that she fell asleep. How could she help doing so when it was so sunny and peaceful by the lake and she had been up most of the night helping Papa to"—The remainder of the speech was lost, as her duenna set silencing fingers on the impetuous lips.

She said quietly, "I accept your very just reprimand, sir, and I also offer apologies for trespass. I will strive to make amends by pointing out to Lucinda that this unpleasant encounter should serve as an object lesson. You can see for yourself, my love, that when wan-

14

dering off unchaperoned one may fall into highly
undesirable company."

The lady had certainly come off with the
honours in *that* encounter, acknowledged his
lordship appreciatively. It was almost a pity
that it must end so soon, since the swift riposte
tempted him to reply in kind, but Miss Pipper,
with an imperative lift of her chin, was already indicating to her charge that it was high
time to withdraw from the scene of battle.

They had reckoned without Miss Lucinda.
That young lady had abandoned her attempts
to invest the afternoon's events with some dramatic excitement and now reverted to her original aim of seeing something of the Merland
ballroom. The pathetic gaze that she directed
at the two antagonists might have drawn tears
from a Grand Inquisitor. Blind to Miss Pipper's
urgent signal—perhaps because the brown eyes
were veiled with the mist of threatened tears—
she very sensibly directed her attack at the
one she judged more vulnerable.

"You should not have scolded Pippa," she
told his lordship sadly. "She had been up all
night helping Stubbs to birth Fantasy's foal.
And now she is cross with you. Won't you say
you are sorry? Because until then I had been
thinking you a very good sort of man, and one
that would perhaps show me the ballroom if I
asked very politely."

His lordship laughed outright. Miss Pipper—

he was still uncertain how to address her—blushed to the roots of her hair and exclaimed crossly, "Lucinda you are quite shameless. Your conduct is pert and presumptuous to the last degree, and must give the most shocking impression of your upbringing," and then, despite herself, joined in his lordship's mirth.

He said unsteadily, "Do you not think that her determination should be rewarded by at least a brief glimpse? I will willingly say that I am sorry for misjudging you—as indeed I am—if that will help matters along. You cannot expect me to forfeit the character of being 'quite a good sort of a man' without at least putting up a fight for it."

Her lips twitched but she said rather anxiously, "Do you think the Marquess would object? It *does* seem to be quite an obsession with her. She has talked about it, dreamed about it, ever since we received our invitation. Perhaps if she could have just one peep—but I would not have you invite censure by giving in to her whims if you think he would dislike it."

"He would not mind in the least," his lordship assured them with perfect truth. "You can see that it would not do to have a great many people in heavy shoes treading on this floor. But two ladies in light slippers are, if I may be permitted a very feeble jest, quite a different pair of shoes. His lordship is a sensible fellow. He would be pleased that Miss Lucinda should enjoy the attractions of his ballroom since she desires it so ardently. Though I fear that there is not a great deal to be seen, which is one of the reasons why the room is usually kept locked." He pulled open the window by which he had attempted his surreptitious exit, and bowed in his most respectful manner to invite the ladies to enter.

It was actually Miss Lucinda who held back. "But your escape," she reminded him anxiously. "Is it wise for you to be lingering here, just to give us pleasure? I *do* dearly long to see the ballroom, but"—

What a nice little creature it was! "At the risk of forfeiting your regard," he said penitently, "I must confess that it was only an escape from a tedious task that I had no inclination to perform."

She nodded quite cheerfully. "I thought it had been something like that. It usually *is* with grown-ups," and walked down the two shallow steps into the ballroom.

Her companion seemed to feel that some explanation was called for. "The trouble is that she has been too much with her elders," she explained apologetically. "In many ways she is old for her years. And since her Mama died she has been a good deal indulged, so that what with her passion for tales of chivalry and derring-do, and her apparent inability to distinguish between make-believe and reality, it is sometimes difficult to know how best to handle her."

His lordship was watching the child's absorbed face as she wandered about the vast room, staring at the classical statues that were placed in some of the alcoves, counting the candleholders in the great chandeliers and climbing the stairs to the musicians' gallery that was hung at one end.

"She is certainly an original," he conceded. "But even on such short acquaintance I would judge her principles to be well established, her disposition affectionate and loyal. She will outgrow the need to make believe"—he smiled at the small, intent figure that was now engrossed in treading out a measure with an imaginary partner—"and become the reigning belle of any ballroom that she chooses to grace with her presence. For if I am not sadly mistaken she shows promise of unusual beauty and undeniable charm."

"Her mother was truly lovely," acknowledged the lady, "and Lucinda is very like her. Sweet-natured, too. But sadly in need of discipline. Yes, I can see that you do not agree with me, but *you* do not have to deal with her romantical starts. She is to go to school next month, and though I shall miss her sorely I think it will do her a great deal of good to mix with other girls of her own age."

His lordship studied her curiously. He suspected that what she had said was good sound sense, but it seemed an unusual attitude for a

18

governess to take. He permitted curiosity to over-rule good manners.

"Are there other children in the family? Or will you be obliged to seek a new situation?"

"There is Dickon," she told him. "He is already at school. But I think you are under a misapprehension. I am Lucinda's cousin, not her governess, though it is true"—her rather plain little face was transformed by a mischievous smile—"that I have endeavoured, without much success, to teach her her lessons since her Mama died. I shall be heartily thankful to be rid of *that* responsibility. She has as many ingenious ways of avoiding the subjects she dislikes as she has of wheedling—er—acquaintances into humouring her fancies."

She glanced at him under her lashes. He was smiling.

"Say strangers, ma'am. We both know that was what you meant. But it was a very harmless fancy, and you should by rights be thanking me instead of raking me down, because now she will give you some peace. I daresay you'll not have a word out of her till bedtime, she will be so busy living in her fantasy world."

"Fantasy!" she exclaimed. "We must go." And then, in hasty explanation, "My uncle's mare. I promised I would look in on her. And indeed, sir, I *am* grateful for your kindness to my little cousin. Most gentlemen, I find, have scant patience with children, even when they are prettily behaved. Your tolerance does you great credit and I would not have you think me unappreciative. Cindy! I promised your Papa that I would go down to the stables to see that all was well with Fantasy and the new foal. Make your adieux without delay."

Apparently Lucinda recognised the voice of authority for she came at once, curtsied, and expressed her thanks in the formal phrases of the well-bred schoolgirl, though the earnest note in her voice and the glow in the big brown eyes lent added sincerity. His lordship disclaimed, declaring that the pleasure had been his—and let the patronising Miss Pipper swallow *that*, the impudent piece, telling him that his kindness did him credit! He then bowed to both ladies in his most distinguished manner and watched them hurry away. The youngster glanced back once and waved a friendly hand, but her cousin was obviously in haste to be gone.

An amusing little interlude. He was glad that they had not known him. It was pleasant to put off for a time the solemn dignity of rank. Though perhaps his little friend would have been pleased and excited if she had guessed the truth. Young enough to believe that there was something glamorous about a title. He grinned suddenly. It seemed highly improbable that her cousin would be of the same opinion.

# Two

Miss Philippa Langley—Pippa to her young cousins—put aside two of Dickon's shirts to be mended and sorted the remainder of the clean linen into orderly piles. It was a dull task and she missed Lucinda's lively chatter. Nor did the grey January day do anything to raise her spirits.

Through the sewing room window she could see bare branches tossing wildly in the icy wind, and abandoned any hope of a short walk to break the monotony of her household duties. No doubt that there were plenty of people who would be thankful to change places with her. She was comfortably established beside a cheerful fire, and quite soon she would be summoned to partake of a savoury, well-cooked meal. Her days were placid and secure—and deadly dull. She would willingly have surrendered something of her comfort for a little variety and excitement. Life had been more cheerful over the Christmas season with both her cousins at home. At least there had been laughter and jokes and teasing. But Lucinda had gone back to school yesterday and Dickon was to leave in two days' time. Her uncle was a dear and she owed him an enormous debt of gratitude, but no one could call him companionable. Particularly at this season of the year when there was a good deal of sickness about. When he was not busy attending to his patients or snatching hurried meals at odd hours because he had missed his dinner, he was usually shut up in his study, pouring over some abstruse medical treatise or compounding remedies of his own devising for common ailments. So long as his household ran smoothly and its inmates were in good health, he did not concern himself further. Lucinda had once declared that she would have to catch smallpox if she wished to be sure of claiming Papa's full attention. Certainly there were whole days when his niece scarcely saw him, and their conversational exchanges were brief and purely practical.

She might not have minded the loneliness so much if her presence had been really essential. But a competent housekeeper could have done all that she did, and Dr. Merchiston was well able to afford the services of such a one. To be sure he made little profit from his medical work, either forgetting to make out a bill or giving his services and advice for nothing if he thought the need was genuine, but fortunately he could do so without hindrance, having inherited a comfortable competence. He had made nothing of taking his orphaned niece into his household, and she had been treated in every respect as though she was his daughter. He was of Scottish descent, strongly imbued with that nation's belief in good education and plain living. It was not until Pippa had attained her twenty first birthday that she learned that she was a considerable heiress in her own right. The money was of little use to her. Her uncle had never accepted a penny for her support and still declined to do so. In his view, his sister's child had a legitimate claim on his hospitality and sheltering care, and that was all there was to be said.

It would have been difficult enough to make a bid for independence in the face of such a debt. With her cousins to think of, it was impossible. She was all they had of the lighter side of home life. Dickon, to his father's strong displeasure, was Army mad. It might be a passing phase—he was not yet sixteen—but Pippa doubted it. And she did not think that his father's acid comments on a career that was devoted to spilling life as opposed to one that was given to saving it, would have much effect. Especially since Dickon, who usually confided in her, had demanded gruffly what was the use of living if—as might well happen—one was enslaved by foreign tyrants? Soldiers, she was given to understand, were just as valuable in such a case as surgeons and physicians.

Lucinda, of course, would marry. With her looks, her engaging personality and a respectable portion she would undoubtedly be a social success, just as the gentleman they had met at Merland had prophesied. Pippa had a little smile for the memory of that summer afternoon. Lucinda had very soon poured out the whole story. The gentleman came out of it pretty well, her cousin thought, and spared a few moments to wonder what was his standing at Merland. Secretary, perhaps. Or steward. At any rate a gentleman in the true sense of the word, if his dealings with Cindy were any criterion.

But Cindy was only fourteen. It would be three years at least before she could be considered marriageable. And by then Pippa Langley would be twenty five and virtually on the shelf. What could the future hold for her? She had money enough to buy herself a husband, she thought, with a cynicism regrettable in one so young, but she did not know that she was particularly interested in husbands. Especially the kind you could buy. She wanted to see something of the world; to stay in London and see the sights; buy pretty clothes and go to the play—oh! a dozen different things that Uncle Philip would condemn as extravagant and frivolous. She was tired of being virtuous and conformable, sick of good works.

She toyed with the thought of foreign travel. Her father had been an incurable wanderer. Not even marriage with her Mama had been able to stifle his longing to discover what lay beyond the next range of hills. Mama, said Uncle Philip, had accompanied him on his travels because it was her duty. But Pippa could just remember her parents and she did not think that duty had had much to say in the matter. Mama had gone gipsying happily enough, thought her daughter, because all she really wanted was to be with Papa. At any rate, their daughter had been given no opportunity of discovering if she had inherited a passion for exploration. Uncle Philip had brought her home to Daylesford when she was seven. Apart from the years that she had spent at school and one or two excursions to such local beauty spots as lay within a day's ride, she had never left it.

Nor could she leave it now, until Dickon and Cindy were settled in life. That would be a fine way to repay Aunt Marion for the affection which had made her own girlhood happy. Cindy in particular needed love. Not cloying sentiment, but understanding, sympathy and, at times, a firm hand on the reins. She was sensitive, and apt to give way to emotional excess. Pippa sighed, and got out her work basket.

A cheerful whistle announced the approach of Cousin Dickon, to inform her that he would be out for luncheon as he meant to take Ruff down to Binns's farm to try for rats in the barn.

"Saw a great big old grand-daddy run in there yesterday," he told her cheerfully. "Papa is gone out, so he won't miss me. I may as well stay at the Binns's. Ned is sure to invite me. To tell you the truth I shall be pretty thankful to be off on Thursday. This place is about as lively as a tomb. I don't know how you can stand it. Why don't you put on your cloak and come down to the farm with me?"

Pippa did not feel that the entertainment suggested was quite to her taste, but she appreciated the kind thought. She declined the invitation and asked her cousin severely if *all* his shirts had the wrist bands torn.

"Most of 'em," he grinned. "They don't show under my jacket," and demonstrated this truth by extending a lanky wrist which protruded a good three inches beyond his cuff.

"I must see about ordering new ones for you," agreed Pippa. "But you're growing so fast it's difficult to get the size right."

Dickon's good-humoured face clouded. "Better if you could order me a new hack," he said bitterly. "I've certainly outgrown Benjy—he's hardly up to Cindy's weight, let alone mine. But all that Papa will say is that until he hears better accounts of my progress in my studies I must put such extravagant notions out of my mind. I wouldn't mind if he really couldn't afford it. And what's more, I *do* work

26

pretty hard. You've got to, if you want to get on in the Army nowadays. It's not enough to be a capital shot and a good horseman, though that's useful too, but I want to serve with the guns, and for that you've got to know mathematics."

He fell into a brooding silence. Pippa felt sorry for him, but could not help hoping that he had not expressed these views to his father. She was thankful when he shook himself out of his dismals and went off, with a recommendation to her not to be screwing up her eyes over sewing, but to find a jolly book to read. There was a copy of Tom Jones on the chest in his room, if she would care for it.

Pippa finished her mending and ate her solitary luncheon before she permitted herself this treat. The day was darkening early, with rain clouds blowing up from the west. She made up the parlour fire and settled down with her book.

She was not allowed to read for long. Dickon's voice was heard shouting for her and the door burst open to admit him, together with his crony, Ned, and a very wet and muddy Ruff, who seemed to be infected by his master's excitement and made explanation both difficult and disjointed by outbursts of hysterical barking.

"... found him half in and half out of the ditch by our ... come a proper ... collar-bone Ned reckons and a crack on hi ... Quiet, Ruff! His horse was lame, too. The poor brute followed us up to the house. Any way, we couldn't leave him there to take his death of cold, so we took the gate off the four-acre and lifted him on to that as carefully as we could. Where shall we put him?"

Having decided that it was the fallen rider and not the horse who was the subject of this enquiry, Pippa suggested that he should be carried into the library, where the gate could be laid on the table. This would save disturbing the patient further until Uncle Philip had ascertained the extent of his injuries. She would have the library fire lit at once, and bricks heated and blankets warmed. The boys could stable the loose horse and see if anything could be done for it.

"And you might shut Ruff up, as soon as you've dried him a bit. I haven't heard half the tale through *that* racket."

She went off to the kitchen to give her orders, and by the time that she returned the two boys, with the assistance of Stubbs, had managed to lift the heavy gate with its unconscious burden on to the table. Water was still trickling slowly from the sodden clothing, and even from the doorway Pippa could see the bruise that disfigured brow and cheek. She wished Uncle Philip would come home. She knew something of the damage that could be done by moving broken bones, but she was strongly of the opinion that the poor man ought to come out of those soaking clothes as soon as possible. She hesitated, nibbling one finger tip anxiously, then made up her mind.

"Dickon, bring me the large scissors out of my work basket, if you please, and one of your Papa's razors for his boots. We must get those wet things off him if he's not to catch his death."

Dickon ran off promptly, but the groom looked shocked. "You can't do that, Miss Philippa. Let alone they boots be worth a mint, 'tain't no work for a young lady."

"And how much will you give for his chances if I'm too ladylike to get him dry and warm," retorted Pippa tartly.

Stubbs tugged sheepishly at his forelock and admitted that maybe she was in the right of it at that, whereupon she, too, relented, explaining that she had not actually intended to undertake the task herself, and urging upon him the importance of reducing the unfortunate gentleman's clothes to shreds rather than 'pulling him about' in an attempt to remove them without damage.

Stubbs nodding his comprehension, she prepared to retreat to the kitchen. "And you may call me as soon as you have him warmly covered," she ended, and felt for a pulse in the cold, rain-sodden wrist, glanced at the still face—and gasped. It was the gentleman of the Merland ballroom.

Some little time elapsed before she was summoned back to the library and her uncle had come home in the meantime, so that she was able to resign the care of the patient into his capable hands. She was a little surprised to find him in such a genial mood when she joined him beside the roaring fire that Stubbs had built up, but it soon emerged that he had been pleased by his son's good sense and capable handling of the situation.

"We shall make a doctor of him yet," he announced, rubbing chilly fingers together in the fire's warmth. "Helped me set that break as handy as you please. This young fellow? Early days to be making guesses. The blow on his head's nothing to cause alarm and the bone's a clean break. But if Dickon hadn't chanced to come across him and bring him in it might have been a different story. All depends on his constitution. Keep him warm and quiet for a day or two, then we'll see. Does any one know who he is?"

"He comes from Merland," said Pippa. "I don't know his name, but he very kindly showed Lucinda and me about when we went to the Public Day last summer."

"We'll send a message over in the morning," decided Uncle Philip. "I'm not turning the horses out again tonight. Get Jenny to sit with him— she's the most sensible—and she can call you if he's restless. I'll mix a paregoric draught and we'll set up a bed here, where it's warm. Soon have him tucked up right and tight."

The patient obligingly recovered consciousness

before the family retired for the night. Jenny reported that he seemed to be in his right senses but disinclined for talk. He had accepted her explanation of his presence in the doctor's house without comment, gazed about him in a rather hazy way and then closed his eyes again. Dickon, who volunteered to sit with him while Jenny ate her supper, found him restless, emerging from a brief doze to enquire abruptly after his horse. The boy's account of the animal's condition and the treatment that Stubbs had advised seemed to satisfy him and he fell into another light sleep.

Dr. Merchiston, visiting him next morning, found him still lethargic and a little feverish but reasonably clearheaded. There was no need to be sending a message to Merland, he insisted. No one would be on the fret for him. If the day's run ended in that direction, he was in the habit of spending the night with a friend who lived near Icomb, and had, in fact, been on his way thither when his horse had come down with him. He could not remember how that had come about. His head, he said ruefully, felt as though it was stuffed with wool. His host assured him that he ailed nothing that could not be set to rights in a day or two with reasonable care, recommended a low diet, but did not think it necessary to bleed him. Moreover he told Pippa that she need no longer set a servant to watch over the young man, since he showed no disposition to behave foolishly. For which dispensation his niece was duly thankful, since there were a dozen last minute items to be stowed in Dickon's trunk before it could be corded ready for the carrier and someone must undertake the various tasks normally performed by Jenny, she having sent the girl to bed. She bade Dickon furnish the sufferer with a hand bell so that he could summon assistance if he should need it, and went off about her morning duties.

She glanced into the library several times in the course of her comings and goings, but on each occasion found the patient resting peacefully with closed eyes. When she had seen Dickon's baggage safely loaded she paid another visit, meaning to discover if he could fancy something a little more substantial than broth. She found her cousin sitting by the bed pouring out a detailed account of the various precautions that he and Stubbs were using to guard against the shocking possibility of the injured animal developing lasting scars. The gentleman's eyes were still closed, but he put in a remark from time to time. However, when Dickon passed on to a rapturous panegyric on the hunter's manifold perfections, Pippa thought it was time to intervene.

"Don't let him tease you, sir. His father prescribed rest and quiet, and very well he knows it. Really, Dickon, I'm surprised at you. You would be better employed in helping Stubbs with those fomentations. This is no time for rhapsodies on blood stock, however gratifying they might be if the listener was in full health. You can see for yourself that he is still a trifle down pin. I apologise for him, sir. In the general way he is perfectly sensible, but the sight of a well-bred horse drives every other consideration out of his head."

Dickon grinned, but had the grace to look slightly shamefaced. "It just shows you that I would never make a doctor," he pointed out defensively. "But I daresay you're right. I beg your pardon, sir."

The sufferer's heavy lids had lifted at the intrusion of the new voice. The grey-blue eyes focussed themselves with some difficulty on the newcomer's face, the straight brows drew together in a slight frown. "But I know you," he said slowly. "I don't recall exactly where we met, but—yes! Of course! Miss Pipper, is it not?"

He seemed quite pleased with himself at this evidence of returning normality. A pleasant smile curved his lips and he held out a hand in greeting. Pippa took it in hers and solemnly shook it, but Dickon's surprised face caused her to say rather primly, "It would be more proper, however, for you to address me as Miss Langley. Pippa is just a pet name that my cousins use."

Comprehension dawned in his lordship's eyes, and with it a faint gleam of amusement. His head still ached abominably but his sense of humour prevailed. "I beg your pardon, ma'am," he said meekly. "I thought it was your surname and intended no familiarity. Your baptismal name, I collect, is Philippa?"

She nodded. "And my cousin is Richard Merchiston, though he prefers to be called Dickon."

His lordship inclined his head. "Quentin Cresswell," he returned, with no thought of deliberate deception. If people did not know that Quentin Cresswell was also the Fifth Marquess of Merland it was scarcely his fault. "Very much at your service. And also of young gabblegrinder here, to whom I understand I owe my rescue. So you must not scold him you know. Besides, as you so rightly surmised, his praise of my Ragamuffin was very sweet."

In face of this courteous attitude Pippa's formality relaxed. She explained her errand, accepted with a good grace the invalid's alarmed rejection of such proffered treats as a morsel of sole baked in milk or the breast of a capon lightly poached in white wine whey, but insisted that he must at least take a little of the supporting broth that had been so carefully prepared, and asked once more if he would not like to send a message to Merland.

He hesitated for a moment. He had his own reasons for not wishing to return to Merland until he could dispense with the services of a nurse, but he did not wish to disclose them to comparative strangers. Yet neither did he wish to impose on their hospitality.

Pippa, wise only in the ways of such as Dickon, saw the hesitation and jumped to an entirely mistaken conclusion.

"Oh dear!" she exclaimed ruefully. "Don't say that you were out without leave. Or is it one of the Marquess's horses that you have lamed? He is in residence, I know, and his love of horses and his pride in his stable are a byword."

It was on the tip of his tongue to explain that he *was* the Marquess, even though the information, in such circumstances, must embarrass all of them. But as he raised himself slightly on the pillows he chanced to catch sight of his reflection in a mirror that was set in the chimney-piece. He was a reasonably modest young man and he would never have expected to be described as handsome. Indeed he took a rather cynical view of his undoubted success with the ladies, ascribing it without hesitation to their interest in his wealth and his rank rather than to the impact of his personal charms. But he had never before seen himself with a disfiguring bruise and a nicely developing black eye in addition to an unshaven chin. When the whole was set off by an ill-fitting flannel night-shirt, property of his kindly host, the effect was ludicrous. For such an apparition to announce pompously that he was a man of high rank was simply impossible. His hearers would be too polite to laugh in his face but they would certainly be hard put to it to refrain.

He sank back again, closing his eyes on the deplorable sight, and said meekly, "No, ma'am, neither of those. But I would rather that no one knew of my mishap just yet. It is asking a good deal, I know; but if you could put up with me for a day or so—just until I have this arm out of its scarf and my colouring, I devoutly trust, a little less startling—I would be most grateful. And I would try not to demand too much of your time and energy."

Both Pippa and Dickon were prompt with assurances of welcome, Dickon loudly bemoaning the fate that would send him back to school just when there was something interesting to do at home. He also undertook to carry a message to Mr. Cresswell's friend, Sir James Waveney, engaging the gentleman's assistance in the task of covering the invalid's protracted absence. His lordship, thankful that it was his left arm that was incapacitated, scrawled a few lines which he trusted would ensure his friend's co-operation, and regretted that he could not offer the loan of his horse for the messenger to ride. Dickon, flushed with pride, scarcely waited for the precise direction of Sir James's house before hurrying off eagerly to serve his new friend.

With Dickon's departure for school the care

of the invalid devolved naturally upon Pippa. And by that time the invalid no longer merited that description. Save for the fact that Dr. Merchiston would not permit him to discard the scarf that supported his left arm and that his bruises were not yet faded, he showed little evidence of his recent mishap. Sir James drove over to visit him, bringing clothes and razors and brushes, and he vacated the library in favour of Dickon's room. Pippa was a little surprised that her uncle tolerated his prolonged visit. One could not call Mr. Cresswell a malingerer. Indeed he more often had to be forbidden some rash activity which would have put undue strain on his injured shoulder. But there could be no denying that he was perfectly well able to go home. However, a private interview between doctor and patient ended with Dr. Merchiston informing his niece that the young fellow could stay as long as he pleased. Since it also caused him to utter sundry mysterious Caledonian ejaculations, quite unintelligible to a Sassenach ear but understood to indicate high good humour, Pippa guessed him to be privy to some secret from which she was excluded and was naturally annoyed. The more so since she could not vent the annoyance on its cause.

Indeed she soon found that she could never be cross with Mr. Cresswell for long. Once his fever had abated Uncle Philip said there was no reason why he should be kept to his bed, and since he confessed that he was not much addicted to reading he soon fell into the habit of tagging along after her as she went about her tasks. It was not long before she was according him about as much formality and respect as she gave to young Dickon. They argued over such diverse topics as the qualities desirable in a hunter—with a brief but spirited digression as to the propriety of ladies taking part in blood sports—to the best ways of keeping honey bees contented and of brewing mead from the fruit of their toil. When Pippa enquired how he came by such odd and distinctly domestic knowledge he refused to say, primming up his lips, the blue-grey eyes laughing at her. When she scolded him for overtaxing his strength in his awkward, one-handed attempts to help her, he would draw such a penitent face that she always ended by laughing with him.

The servants liked him, which made her task as housekeeper easier, since they hastened to do whatever he wished and even to forestall his requests. And it was not just because he was generous with money. She knew that he *was*, because Dickon had come to her saucer-eyed to show the guineas that had been thrust upon him when he went to bid Mr. Cresswell goodbye, asking if he might properly accept them. She had assured him that two guineas was just the sort of tip that an indulgent uncle might well bestow upon a favoured nephew who was about to return to the rigours of the educational system, and could in no sense be construed as an attempt to reward him for his recent services, and a much relieved Dickon had gone off happily, debating on the most profitable ways of investing his unexpected largesse.

Pippa was shrewd enough to reckon that this careless generosity stemmed from affluence. Mr. Cresswell had never had to make one shilling do the work of two, nor suffered any deprivation because he had given away the price of a meal. That did not make it any less creditable. Not every wealthy man was generous—and she had decided that Mr. Cresswell was comfortably circumstanced rather than wealthy, the simplicity of his manners and his total lack of self consequence confirming her in this naive belief.

It took the better part of a week for the bruises to fade to insignificance, and by that time their friendship had advanced to the stage of easy intimacy. They had exchanged the more memorable incidents in their respective histories and compared tastes and prejudices. Mr. Cresswell had heard, with respectful sympathy, that Pippa's parents had died in an Indian raid. They had come, in their wanderings, to Boone County in distant Kentucky. Mama's letters to her brother, with their excited accounts of the discovery of the bones of huge pre-historic animals, had tempted sober, stay-at-home Uncle Philip to make the long journey to see for himself. So it had come about that he had been at hand to bring the orphaned Philippa home to England.

"So you see I owe him more than I can ever repay," she explained. "Now do you understand why I can't just abandon my cousins to the loneliness of a motherless home?"

They had clashed on this head before. Pippa had been unable to listen to Mr. Cresswell's stories of Town life and of a leisurely Grand Tour without betraying something of the envy and frustration that filled her. While admitting that her sex made foreign travel difficult he had said that surely she must have some respectable female relative who could introduce her into the world of fashion. He had raised a disbelieving eyebrow when she said that she knew of none, especially when she added that even if she did, she would not apply to her. Reluctantly he admitted that her story silenced, even if it did not satisfy him.

Had he but known it, his coming had dispelled Pippa's restlessness. She had never been so busy nor so well amused in years. She had little notion of feminine wiles and none at all of her own pretensions to beauty, so she did not dress to please him, but she found herself planning especially tempting meals and waiting eagerly for a word of appreciation, or searching her memory for some amusing incident that would make him smile. She reflected hopefully that Merland was not so very far away. This delightful new friendship need not come to an abrupt end with his going. Perhaps they could persuade him to join them in some of their simple excursions during the summer holidays. Both Dickon and Lucinda would be over the moon with joy, and his companionship would be particularly good for Dickon. She smiled contentedly at the thought, and had not the least idea that she was already more than half in love with him.

Meanwhile she sang as she worked, her pretty laughter rang out with unusual frequency, and she greeted each new day with delight and no thought of the morrow.

# Three

But the day inevitably came when the supporting scarf was discarded, his host announced that as an invalid he was a complete fraud, and Sir James was to drive over next day to carry him back to Icomb.

Pippa could not help regretting the imminence of his departure, however much she rejoiced in his swift recovery. Life would be very dull without him. Her every day tasks had taken on a new aspect because of his amused curiosity, his teasing and his enthusiastic, if awkward, assistance. She went with him to the stables to watch while he groomed Ragamuffin for the last time, her spirits unaccountably low. It had been arranged that the horse should remain at Doctor's Lodge until he was fit enough to be ridden gently back to Merland. Surely that was pledge enough that she would see his master again before so many days had passed.

They talked horses with enthusiasm. So easy were they grown together that Pippa spoke quite freely about Dickon's desire for a mount more suited to his build and aptitude than stolid, comfortable old Benjy. Quentin eyed the placid brown gelding thoughtfully and agreed that if Dickon's legs grew much longer they would touch the ground when he bestrode the poor beast, but suggested that it would be something of a problem to keep a suitable mount properly exercised while Dickon was away at school.

"I daresay I could find him something to ride in the holidays," he said. "I'll have a word with his father before I go."

Pippa rather doubted if the suggestion would find favour but the kindly thought did much to hearten her. She brushed the loose hairs from her skirt and said that she must go and change her dress before luncheon.

As she neared the side door which was the most conveniently placed for the stables, it was flung open abruptly and Jenny came hurrying out, her cap askew, her face flushed and excited. "Oh, Miss Philippa!" she exclaimed breathlessly. "Please will you come. There's a lady asking for you. A Lady Merland."

"Goodness!" exclaimed Pippa. "It must be the Dowager, for the young man isn't married. I daresay she has come to enquire for Mr. Cresswell. But I really can't hob-nob with the aristocracy with my dress in this state. Where did you put her?"

"I left her in the hall, miss. Mrs. Stubbs is polishing the library floor and I never thought to ask her to step upstairs to the parlour. I was proper put about to find myself talking to a real live ladyship."

Pippa groaned. "Whatever will she think of us? Go back at once and show her into the parlour. Send someone to call Mr. Cresswell, and do you offer her refreshment. Tell her Miss Langley has just stepped out but is expected back at any moment," and fled up the back stairs, unbuttoning her well-worn merino as she went.

She poured water from the ewer and washed her hands and face, shuddering a little at the cold bite of it. But at least it brought colour to her cheeks, and the soft, rose-coloured kerseymere that she hurriedly selected was one of her more becoming gowns, though it was plain enough and of country cut. A glance through the window as she brushed her hair confirmed her conjecture as to the visitor's identity. The coachman was dutifully walking his horses and the gleaming carriage bore an unmistakeable dowager's lozenge.

She was not particularly over-awed by Lady Merland's exalted rank. She supposed that her ladyship had called to express her thanks for the hospitality shown to her young employee,

45

which was always rather an awkward business, and made worse on this occasion by the unfortunate circumstances of the lady's reception. Nevertheless it was with a reasonable degree of composure that she presently made her way to the first floor parlour.

It was a pleasant, comfortable apartment, if a trifle shabby. Aunt Marion had loved it because it had windows in two walls and so caught the sunlight for most of the day. No wonder the hangings and cushions were faded, thought Pippa as she pushed open the door. And today, lacking the sunshine, lacking Aunt Marion's welcoming warmth, the room was not at its best. Nor did the lady who was apparently subjecting its furnishings to a critical appraisal do anything to lighten the atmosphere.

She was a little above average height and built on noble lines, her features handsome, her expression one of cool civility that yet conveyed a hint of secret amusement. Her carriage dress was black, save for the lace at throat and wrists, but there was nothing about its restrained elegance to suggest the inconsolable widow. It seemed rather designed to complement raven locks and a creamy skin, while its masculine cut served to accentuate a natural arrogance that was revealed in every gesture and movement. Even as Pippa came in, her uninvited guest raised a long-handled eye-glass which hung from a riband about her neck and used it to examine a sampler that hung on the wall; a sampler that a ten-year-old Philippa had stitched lovingly, if rather crookedly, as a gift for Aunt Marion. Gentlemen frequently used such glasses, but Pippa had never seen a lady do so. She guessed the glass to have been specially made. It was smaller than its masculine counterpart, the ebony handle set with sparkling stones. Diamonds, supposed Pippa; a wealthy lady's toy. She was diverted, even a little fascinated, but not unduly impressed. Her visitor was like something out of a story book, a little larger than life. Pippa was prepared to be polite and hospitable and to savour to the full this fantastic little interlude in her orderly days. For that was all it was. Very soon the lady would be gone.

The creak of the closing parlour door revealed her presence. The marchioness turned with leisurely grace and bestowed a delightful smile upon her.

"Miss Philippa Langley?" she enquired.

Pippa curtsied.

Her ladyship, very much mistress of the situation, indicated the sampler with a gesture of the quizzing glass and murmured, "Charming. Quite charming! But a trifle injudicious, do you not think?" And then, seeing Pippa's air of puzzlement, said lightly, "It is all very well when 'Philippa Langley, Aged Ten Years' and the present date, taken together, proclaim that you are no more than two or three and twenty. But how will it be in ten years' time? You will

47

not then be so eager to announce your age to every chance guest!"

Pippa laughed. It was really too ridiculous. Everyone in the vicinity knew perfectly well how old she was. It was impossible to keep such a secret when half a dozen daughters of local families had shared one's schooldays. And what could it possibly matter? If reticence about a girl's age was a social requirement in the aristocracy, then there was something to be said for rustic obscurity.

"But it would be a sad pity to unpick stitches so laboriously set," she returned, smiling, and went on to apologise for the delay in welcoming her ladyship, explaining that she had been in the stables, "—my dress all covered with Ragamuffin's hairs," and had been obliged to change it before she was fit to be seen.

Her ladyship wore a very thoughtful expression as she assessed the clear, pretty voice, the unaffected manners, the easy bearing. Miss Langley was not quite what she had expected. Passably good looking, too, though she did not know how to make the most of her figure and even at this season of the year the fair skin still showed faintly freckled. Never one to underrate an adversary—or perhaps, in this case, a minor irritant—Lady Merland decided that instinct had served her aright in prompting her to enquire for herself into the circumstances in which her unpredictable nephew was passing his convalescence. Why he could not have had himself conveyed to Merland was more than she could understand. Every care and luxury at his command—she and Flora would have been delighted to keep him amused and entertained—but no! He must needs prefer what, to her ladyship, was practically squalor. Perhaps the reason was standing here before her, politely urging her to partake of ratafia and sweet biscuits. Or there was orgeat if she would prefer that.

Quentin was a fool, decided his aunt dispassionately, accepting a glass of ratafia. He should know better than to meddle with the genteel middle classes. The girl and her family would be grossly insulted if he offered her a carte blanche. They would not understand such affairs. And marriage, of course, was out of the question. Such disparity in rank and fortune could never be reconciled, even if her ladyship had not harboured certain plans of her own about a suitable match for her nephew.

She made easy small talk, discussing the prospects for skating and asking if Miss Langley meant to attend the Hunt Ball next month, and all the while the acute mind behind the social mask was pondering the degree of the threat posed by this interloper, debating the best means of countering it. A puzzled Pippa sustained her part in this exchange without undue effort, but wished her ladyship would come to the point. She was already a good deal behind with her morning's tasks.

And presently even her ladyship's facile invention came to an end. She declined further refreshment and rose, saying coolly, "But I must not be lingering here, keeping you from your work, though I have enjoyed our little chat. I came only to thank you for your hospitality to my nephew and to discover how best we can recompense you for all the expense and trouble to which you have been put."

Coming at the end of twenty minutes during which hostess and caller had met on equal, even friendly terms, the impact of this careless patronage was severe. The close relationship between Lady Merland and Mr. Cresswell meant nothing to Pippa, who did not even know that Cresswell was the Merland family name, and the insolent offer of payment for the hospitality which had been so freely given was more than she could meekly accept. She drew herself up very straight and looked her ladyship full in the face as she said quietly, "On that head, ma'am, you must address yourself to my uncle. Hospitality and expense alike are his. I am concerned only in so far as I have carried out his wishes."

Her ladyship, unaccustomed to such plain speaking, was a little taken aback. She shifted her ground slightly.

"My apologies, child," she murmured with languid sweetness. "I see I have offended. But indeed you must not be so swift to take offence.

And though the *expense* of my nephew's stay falls on your worthy uncle, I am sure that the *care* of him fell to your lot."

"And in so far as it did, ma'am, it was my pleasure," retorted Pippa swiftly.

"I see." Her ladyship permitted herself a reflective smile and her gaze roved deliberately over the girl's face and figure, her amusement growing visibly. "Yes. I do indeed see. But— forgive me, my dear. Was that quite wise? You are young"—she nodded briefly at the sampler —"and quite unsophisticated. For your own protection I must speak frankly. Quentin is a very charming young man—as several other young ladies would undoubtedly agree. No doubt you have enjoyed a delightful little flirtation, perfectly innocent and harmless. But it cannot continue. You are a good girl, I feel sure, if a little foolish and misguided. A period of rational reflection must convince you that nothing but shame and disgrace can come of an association where there is such disparity of rank."

Pippa frankly stared. No thought of romance or flirtation had entered into her dealings with Mr. Cresswell. She had treated him much as she treated Dickon, though naturally she had enjoyed his society in a different way because he was older, widely travelled and well informed. As for disparity of rank—and here her anger rose. Who were the Merlands, that this overbearing, patronising female should openly

51

despise a girl who could trace her ancestry in the direct line for three hundred years and more? It was unfortunate and probably unfair that Quentin, because of his Merland blood, should be included in her anger. She was even dimly aware of this. It helped her to keep face and voice in control as she said stiffly, "You are very concerned for my welfare, ma'am, but your warnings are quite unnecessary. I think you came here, not to express gratitude for kindness shown to your nephew but to interfere in matters which are no concern of yours. I find your intrusion ill-bred and quite unacceptable, and so I will bid you farewell. If you choose to await your nephew's coming—one of the servants went to summon him—you may do so."

Not since she emerged from the schoolroom had any one addressed Lady Merland in such outspoken reproof. Fury almost choked her. It vibrated in a voice from which every trace of languid sweetness had vanished.

"Why! You insolent hussy!" she exclaimed. "Do you *really* imagine that you will hold your place in his lordship's easy affections in face of *my* disapproval? Or perhaps you even dreamed of marriage. Little fool! Marquesses don't marry village maidens. But if you are so eager to join the ranks of the muslin company, it is, as you say, no concern of mine. Give you good-day, Mistress Langley. Your fate is on your own head."

At which singularly inopportune moment his lordship walked into the room.

He had not hurried unduly over changing his stablescented garments for attire more suited to a lady's drawing room. He was annoyed because his aunt had discovered his whereabouts, even more so that she should have sought him out there, and foresaw an awkward, stilted interview in which she would use all the consequence of her rank to overawe and crush his defenceless little hostess. He came in warily, but unprepared to deal with a Philippa who was a stranger to him. A Philippa white-faced and furious, who had just suffered a shocking enlightenment as to his true identity. His aunt also looked distinctly out of temper, yet at the same time a trifle smug.

She had good cause for smugness. Her thinking reference to a fact with which she had supposed Miss Langley to be already acquainted had driven a rift between the pair far more effective than anything that she had achieved by her earlier efforts. Pippa felt that she had been deliberately deceived and made to look foolish. His lordship was sorry for her distress but could not feel that his deception was so very bad. Nor could he explain, in front of his aunt, just how it had come about. In any case he was given no opportunity to do so.

"I am sure you will hold me excused," said Miss Langley, very much on her dignity. "I have much to do. A humble establishment must marshall its resources with care when it entertains so noble a guest. Perhaps you will be so good, milord, as to inform Mrs. Waring if you wish to make any changes in your arrangements."

On which reprehensibly youthful note, she left them to their own devices.

# *Four*

It was to be months before Pippa could recall
that unpleasant scene without feeling the rush
of painful colour to her cheeks. Her brief attempt
at sarcasm was regretted almost as soon as it
was uttered. She knew that it betrayed a childish resentment and was quite as bad as anything that Lady Merland had said. But also, in
some inexplicable way, it hurt *her* rather than
the Merlands.

For the rest of the day she had kept to her
room. Cowardly, she acknowledged, but her
wounds were still too raw to endure even the
light armour of the social façade. Alone she had
fought the painful battle for acceptance and
composure, hearing the sound of voices on the
terrace below, the closing of a door and the
departure of the Merland carriage without so
much as raising her head.

Uncle Philip had tapped at her door to enquire
what ailed her that she had been absent from

both lunch and dinner, and when she had said that she was perfectly well but just a little tired he had reproved her for self indulgence and discourtesy to their guest. That had been the last straw. She had given way to such a storm of weeping that the poor man had been sadly disconcerted. Philippa! His sensible, practical Philippa, who had never cried, even as a child, except once when a marauding terrier had so mauled her pet rabbit that he had been obliged to put the poor creature out of its misery. And even then she had lifted a face still smeary with tears and gravely thanked him. He let her sob herself out against his shoulder, and obliged her to swallow a mild sedative draught before he enquired further into the cause of this distress. Philippa was unpractised in the art of dissimulation. In any case there was nothing to hide. She gave him a truthful account of the morning's disastrous interview, punctuated by an occasional choke in the soft voice as she caught her breath on a strangled sob. Only at the very end did her gaze waver and avoid his. It was with a shamed face that she confessed to her own rash retort, but she told it truthfully and made no plea in extenuation.

His response had been swift. "That was wrong in you," he said soberly. "His lordship had done nothing to merit such an unkind set-down. And in administering it in such a crude fashion you shamed your own blood."

She nodded meekly. "I know. I deeply regret it. Do you think that I should apologise, or would that be to make too much of so small a matter?"

He shook his head rather ruefully. "In any case it is too late. His lordship has already retired, since he proposes to leave betimes tomorrow. He means to attend the meet at Icomb. I warned him that that shoulder of his won't stand up to any more punishment for a few weeks, but he only laughed and said that he would probably not go beyond the first few fields but that he must make a beginning some time."

"You think that he wishes to avoid meeting me again?" suggested Pippa soberly.

"Say rather that he wishes to spare you embarrassment," returned her uncle. She coloured unhappily, but she was able to take some comfort from his indignation over Lady Merland's insinuations, even if she could not wholly agree with him that the opinion of such a contemptible creature was not worth a straw.

"One can scarcely call her contemptible," she objected doubtfully. "She is a woman of high rank, and well versed, one must suppose, in all social matters."

The doctor snorted. "And what good does she do in the world? From what I can make out she is wholly given over to worldly considerations, with no higher ambition than to lead society by the nose and to arrange a fashionable marriage for her nephew."

Pippa eyed him suspiciously. "You seem to know a great deal about them," she ventured, and then, as he did not immediately answer, "Oh no! Never say that you knew all along that he was Lord Merland. Is *that* why you agreed to his staying on here? I find it hard to believe."

"As well you may! Don't throw your tongue at me, my girl. You've done enough damage in that line already, today. You've had a trying morning, so I'll forgive your impertinence this once. But you should know perfectly well that it's no such thing. The first time I saw that young man I knew no more than you did who he was. He was a patient. And I'd have done as much for a tinkler lad in like case. But when he asked if he could stay on a few days he made a clean breast of it. Seems he'd had a hard enough task shifting his lady aunt out of Merland and installed in the Dower House. There's been one excuse after another to delay matters. He reckoned if he went back home with so much as a trace of the invalid about him, she'd be back before the cat could lick her ear and it would all be to do again. Also there's some niece or cousin staying with her whom she's trying to foist on to him as a suitable bride. In face of a determined assault of that kind, a decent lad's pretty helpless. He can't say what he thinks without being downright rude. The only thing he can do is run. And since you can't run very far with a broken collar bone and a touch of concussion, the next best thing is to lie low. Which is why he wanted to stay here until he could get about more freely. But I'd like to know who let it out that he was here, for there wasn't another soul in the house who knew who he really was. Not that it matters much now, but I'd not like him to think that *I* was responsible."

"Perhaps it came from Sir James Waveney or from one of his household," suggested Pippa. "But I cannot help wishing that you had let *me* into the secret. I have never in my life felt so small and so silly."

"Then you're a fool, my girl. Your birth is as good as his, and no need of titles to proclaim it. It's not every title that a man can be proud to bear. Look back in history. There's more than one that was ennobled for his *wife's* services to the Monarch, or for doing some dirty work that suited the royal interest. Not that I'm saying there's aught wrong with young Merland. Indeed I liked him pretty well and was happy to do him a service. As for telling you—I never thought about it. And just as well, it seems to me, the pother you're making. If you'd known, you'd never have been done fretting over whether the food was to his liking and the linen fine enough."

Pippa denied this charge indignantly, and felt the better for doing so. But secretly she knew that there was a germ of truth in it. Perhaps she would not have been unduly concerned over her hospitality, since any guest at Doctor's Lodge was given the best that the establishment could provide. But certainly she would not have found it so easy to be natural and friendly. She was not quite sure whether that was good or bad, but her uncle's matter-of-fact manner and his unconscious assertion of equality with the Merlands had done much to calm and strengthen her. She meekly accepted his recommendation of a bowl of oatmeal gruel to stay an empty stomach and a hot brick to her feet to induce sound sleep, but despite her improved state of mind she was still thankful that she would not be obliged to see his lordship again.

She slept only fitfully and went about the next day's work in a very desultory way. Life was dull; the future devoid of promise. She trailed about disconsolately, unable to settle to any of her usual pastimes, now bitterly ashamed as she recalled what had passed between herself and Lady Merland, now seething with resentment that she had been kept in ignorance of Mr. Cresswell's true identity. All her troubles, she felt, stemmed from that withheld confidence. If only she had known, she would have treated him with far more circumspection; would not have been unprepared for Lady Merland's attack. Certainly she would never have admitted him so far into her friendship that now she missed his company in everything she did. This last, of course, she did not acknowledge. Instead she told herself how fortunate it was that she had discovered his perfidy so early in their acquaintance, and went off to tidy the drawers in her dressing chest, quite pleased with her own calm good sense.

Unfortunately she very soon discovered that this quality was perilously fragile. She had not half finished her self-imposed task when the sound of wheels approaching the house sent her scampering to the window, shedding a trail of gloves, stockings and handkerchieves in her wake. She was just too late to catch a glimpse of the caller, who, obviously familiar with the house, had driven straight into the stable yard.

Her heart was beating furiously and a swift glance in the mirror to ensure that she was tidy enough to receive visitors showed a heightened colour. But she was determined that she would receive him in a perfectly civil and collected fashion with no sign of the disapproval that his deception merited. It was therefore a sad disappointment when Jenny came running upstairs to tell her that Sir James Waveney had called and would be glad of a few words with her if the time was convenient.

Since Lady Merland's visit, Philippa had become very conscious of the awkwardness of her situation when receiving male guests. It had never previously occurred to her, or to Uncle Philip, that she was too young to do so without a chaperone. Besides, until the advent of his lordship, the only male guests had been friends of Dickon's, and were too young to give grounds for scandalous conjecture. But she hesitated only briefly. If Lady Merland was in the right of it her reputation was already past praying for, so she might just as well receive Sir James and discover his errand. She smoothed her hair, took a clean handkerchief, and went down to the library.

Sir James, several years younger than his lordship, seemed a trifle ill at ease. He was an amiable young man, not over-burdened with brains. So much Philippa had recognised at their first meeting. He was quite at home on any sporting suit, but if obliged to carry out any mission requiring tact or initiative he liked to have his instructions repeated two or three times. Consequently she was not particularly surprised to learn that it was he who had inadvertently given away the secret of his friend's whereabouts.

"She'd driven out with that chit she's got staying with her to watch the draw at Pook's Coppy. Can always be sure of a find there. And comes smash up to me to ask why Quentin wasn't out. 'Fraid I was more concerned with watching hounds and getting a good start. Came out with the truth before I remembered he wanted it kept dark. 'N of course she was on to it like a hawk. Can't think why people *will* come out to see the hunt. They're always a pesky nuisance. Kept me talking for nigh on ten minutes so that I missed a first rate gallop and never caught up till they checked in Gallaber Bottoms. As well as spoiling all my pleasure, because every time hounds were brought to their noses I'd be remembering that I'd betrayed Quentin to that old harridan. Which she is, Miss Langley. Well—not precisely old, perhaps, but certainly a harridan. Because she harries the poor fellow until he can't call his home his own."

He paused for breath at the end of what was, for him, a long and lucid explanation, and looked about him in a vague sort of way as though he was not quite sure of his whereabouts or his errand. The sight of a large rush basket, distinctly out of place on the library table, recalled his wandering wits.

"I took the liberty of driving round to the stables, Miss Langley," he said apologetically. "There were one or two things that Quentin asked me to bring over for your uncle. Thought I'd best go to the servants' entrance," he added with a feeble attempt at humour. Then, awkwardly, "Thing is, you see, Quentin's the best of good fellows. Didn't rail at me for letting the cat out of the bag. Least I could do to come over here on his behalf. Still in queer stirrups, y'know. Quite done up this morning. Tried to make him rest, but no. Nothing would do for him but to go over to Merland to get some things he wanted. Went with him, of course. Couldn't let him go alone in that state. Even missed the meet." He paused for a moment in naive admiration of his own self sacrifice, but returned doggedly to his exposition. "Glad to do anything for a friend, of course, 'specially after making such a mull of the other business, but felt bound to tell him diplomacy's not much in my line. Only hope I don't make a mull of *this*. He said you was as mad as fire over something his aunt had said to you. These"—he picked up the basket—"are to make his apology—or was it his peace with you? I forget. Always a bit of a slow-top y'know. Oh yes! I left the port and the pheasants in the kitchen." He heaved a sigh of relief for the conclusion of his delicate and difficult task, and awaited Miss Langley's comments with hopeful interest.

The basket contained a great armful of pink tulips, their buds still tightly folded. On this cold January day they were very beautiful, holding out the promise of spring, even though their very perfection revealed that they were the product of some sheltered, heated succession house. Pippa surveyed them woodenly. The very lavishness of the offering smacked, to her, of charity. Taken in conjunction with the mention of pheasants and wine they were too much for that touchy pride of hers, still sore from yesterday's humiliation.

"His lordship is most generous," she said, face and voice so totally lacking in animation that even Sir James realised that something was wrong. He puzzled over it for a full minute

64

and was rewarded by an idea of surpassing brilliance.

"If you was to write him a note," he offered eagerly, "I could carry it back for you. I don't mind waiting. Stubbs said he'd see to my horses, so they'll take no hurt. A good man, Stubbs."

A pretty note of thanks was the last thing in Pippa's mind, but she could no more have refused that ingenuous plea than she could have punished a penitent pup that did not know just how it had erred. She told him that her writing materials were in her own room, but that if he would hold her excused for a quarter of an hour she would certainly do as he suggested, and hurried away, so intent on devising the acid phrases with which she would scarify his lordship that she did not notice Sir James's look of dismay when she suggested that he find a book from the library shelves with which to pass the time.

The composition of the note took longer than she had thought, though to be sure it was brief enough after she had torn up half a dozen attempts in which indignation broke through the polite phrases. She finally informed Lord Merland—in the third person because she was not quite sure how one should address a Marquess—that Miss Langley thanked him for his generous gifts and was sure that her uncle would much appreciate the game birds and the wine. The flowers were very pretty. She had decided to send them to Mrs. Verney—the vicar's wife—to be used in the adornment of the church.

It was not as scathing as she would have liked. She would really have preferred to return the gifts, but *that* Uncle Philip would never permit. At least she had made it abundantly clear that *she* would have nothing to do with them. She sealed the note with a sense of fierce satisfaction and carried it down to the library to find her messenger peacefully asleep in front of the fire and full of embarrassed apology when she was obliged to rouse him.

The satisfaction did not last very long. His lordship made no further overtures, so her decision to meet any such approach with a forceful snub was rather wasted. The weeks passed. The steady routine of her days was resumed. There might never have been a teasing, mischievous young man to disturb their even tenor. All too soon her anger abated. Before the first week was out she was ready to admit that she had been unfair, releasing the anger aroused by Lady Merland on the head of her unfortunate nephew. And without the support of her anger she began to feel very low and forlorn, though self respect obliged her to maintain a cheerful front.

Worse trials lay ahead. Having once adopted this attitude of unapproachability, it was impossible to abandon it. How could one possibly write and say that one regretted the discourtesy with which his flowers had been rejected. Every instinct rebelled. And just imagine Lady Merland's comments! So when holidays brought Dickon and Lucinda home again, she found herself in an awkward fix. For his lordship did not, as she had half expected, forget that last comfortable conversation that they had enjoyed in the stable. He wrote to Uncle Philip suggesting that a couple of his hacks should be put at Dickon's disposal during the holiday, and acceptance of this kindly offer led naturally to occasional meetings between the boy and his benefactor. In August his lordship played host to a lively party of young people— relatives and their friends, who enjoyed the amenities of Merland just as he himself had done in days gone by. Dickon was invited to join in some of their excursions and seemed to spend more time at Merland than at home. Presently the invitations were extended to include Pippa and Cindy. The latter was ecstatic. Ever since she had learned that her 'ballroom gentleman' was none other than the marquess himself, she had been in a glow of romantic adoration. She was for ever plying Dickon with questions as to just how his lordship had looked and exactly what he had said and done, and Dickon, also far sunk in hero worship, was only too ready to oblige. And since, for some reason, Pippa found it impossible to turn a deaf ear to any scrap of fresh information as to the gentleman's tastes and activities, it was difficult to maintain the air of cool detachment on which she had decided.

The invitation to join the Merland party on a whole day's riding picnic was the last straw. Dickon, who had taken their delighted acceptance for granted, had already described all the arrangements to his sister, and to be obliged to forego such a splendid treat just because Pippa thought it was too far and reminded her that overexertion in this heat was likely to bring on one of the megrim headaches to which she was subject, was too bad to be endured. She need not ride all the way—could make the homeward journey in the pony carriage which was to convey the picnic hampers to the chosen spot. Dickon supported her—was sure his lordship would not object to so simple a compromise—but Pippa was firm. Cindy could not be roving all over the countryside without a chaperone, and to ask one of the other guests to go with her in the pony carriage was unthinkable. She herself did not intend to accept his lordship's invitation. Such juvenile affairs, she said rashly, were no longer her notion of a high treat.

That naturally inclined Dickon even more strongly to his sister's side. He pointed out that at least two of the guests were older than his cousin and one of them was a married lady, too. But of course if she felt herself to be getting old cattish it was not for him to disagree with her. He actually offered to drive home with Cindy in the pony cart, a chivalrous gesture that caused his sister to dissolve into floods of tears and to vow, between her sobs, that not for worlds would she spoil her dear Dickon's enjoyment of the party.

So much had the management of her young cousins been left to Pippa, that she never dreamed that Cindy would carry her troubles to her father. She was completely taken aback when Uncle Philip strolled out into the garden where she was weeding a rose bed and said mildly, "What's this tale of Lucinda's about not being able to go to Lord Merland's picnic without a chaperone? Since she's not yet sixteen I would have thought that your society and her brother's might have been reckoned more than adequate to the occasion."

Pippa flushed. "I had decided not to go," she said rather awkwardly. "And although Dickon offered to drive with his sister, she would not hear of it, saying that it would spoil the party for him."

"As indeed it would," nodded the doctor. "But what ails *you*, child, that you do not wish to go?"

Pippa embarked on a very lame explanation about not wishing to spend a whole day with a party of strangers, and of having a great deal to do at home, with the raspberries and black-currants all ripening together.

Dr. Merchiston eyed her shrewdly. "If that is the truth, it seems that I have been sadly remiss in the manner of your upbringing," he said. "It is natural enough for a young woman to be a little shy of strangers. To be going to such lengths to avoid meeting them is not. As for household duties, there are servants enough to attend to those—or if there are not, we may engage more. I do not wish to interfere with your management or to weaken your authority, but the child does not have many treats and this one seems to me quite unexceptionable. As for your prejudice against strangers, are you sure that it is not the thought of meeting one particular gentleman who is *not* a stranger that has caused you to put a few pots of preserves before your cousin's pleasure? For such a choice is most unlike you."

"It is true that I would prefer not to meet Lord Merland," said Pippa stiffly, "but it is equally true that I think the ride would be too far for Cindy in this heat."

Cindy's father nodded thoughtfully. "That's my good honest girl. But no more nonsense about jampots and shyness if you please. If you do not care for the expedition, Lucinda may perfectly well go with the Verneys. I understand that Marcia has been invited to join the party and do not doubt that Mrs. Verney will be quite willing to take charge of Lucinda as well." He read the relief in Pippa's face, but he was not yet quite done with her. "Pride can be a costly luxury," he said slowly. "And it can grow and grow until it distorts your vision and

70

your judgement. Root it out, girl, like these dandelions." He stirred the heap of weeds with his toe, and went back into the house.

Nevertheless, in spite of her uncle's sage advice, that same prickly pride drove Pippa to spend the day of the Merland picnic in the fruit garden. The occupation gave a little substance to her excuses, but it did not do much to distract her thoughts from the delights that Cindy and Dickon would be enjoying. Delights which, despite her denials, she longed to share. If only, without lowering the flag of her pride, she could somehow resume the old, friendly relationship. She had long forgotten any sense of injury. It was just the difficulty of making the first move.

She sighed, tipped the contents of her basin into the large bowl that stood at the end of the row, and decided that there was just time to strip one more bush before she must go in to change her gown for supper. The picnic party would be home soon. There would be a whole evening of joyous reminiscence to be endured.

She had her head and arms thrust into the heart of a blackcurrant bush, seeking the fat black berries that always grew in the most inaccessible places, when she heard the click of the garden gate. Thinking only that it was Jenny, come to summon her to supper, she called, "I won't be a moment. You may carry the bowl up to the house."

There was a brief pause. Then a deep, amused

voice said, "Willingly. But there is surely no great haste? I can wait until you are quite done."

Pippa backed out of her leafy refuge with more haste than grace, emerging with wildly ruffled hair and blue-stained fingers and lips, where one or two prime specimens had been popped into her mouth. Drat the man! Once again the strategic advantage lay with him.

But there was no real displeasure in the thought. As Lady Merland had surmised, Pippa had never given much consideration to her own appearance, and she did not do so now. He was here. He had made the first move. Only, perhaps—

"Is all well?" she asked swiftly. "Cindy? She was not overcome by the heat?"

"Cindy was in high gig when last I saw her," he returned. "I left her at the Verney's. Mrs. Verney said that one of the abigails would walk home with her. No, it was young Marcia who was sick. Over-indulgence in creams and pastries—or so her hard-hearted Mama declared—and she seems quite recovered. But in view of what Dickon had told me I thought it was probably wiser to include Cindy in the party. So you may stop fussing, Mother Hen— though goose would be more appropriate—and permit me to remove the caterpillar which is just about to embark on an exploration of your right ear."

She gave a little shriek and put up a hand to

her hair. He stooped and detached the obliging little creature that had presented him with just the light-hearted impersonal touch that he had desired. For a moment he held it on his hand so that she could see for herself that it was no hoax, then carefully replaced it on a leaf.

"Now it will go and lay hundreds of eggs and the poor bush will be eaten alive," said Pippa, trying hard to sound indignant and finding it very difficult in face of the warm tide of happiness that was rising within her. "You should have trodden on it."

"Your education, my child, has been sadly neglected. Caterpillars don't lay eggs. And I wouldn't have trodden on that particular specimen for twenty golden guineas."

He eyed her quizzically. But Pippa, suddenly shy, did not enquire why he set such a value on a mere caterpillar. Instead she asked, rather diffidently, if he would not come in and take a glass of wine.

His answer set the seal on her contentment. "If you will tell me that you no longer hold me in dislike, either on account of my aunt's abominable behaviour, or, more probably, my own, I will be very happy to do so," he said soberly.

The happiness in her face and the eager decisive nod were answer sufficient. He held out his hands and she put hers into them. Quentin said mischievously, "Do you remember how you used to coax me to drink my chicken broth, or to swallow various vile potions that you insisted would do me a great deal of good? I cannot help feeling that if you were to exert your persuasive powers I might even consent to stay to supper."

If Pippa had entertained any last lingering doubts about the awkwardness of friendship with a gentleman of superior station, this audacious suggestion banished them for all time. She laughed and led the way into the house. And supper, though it consisted only of cold meats and various salads, somehow became a feast. Both Dickon and Cindy vowed that they could not eat another morsel, so replete as they were with picnic fare. Pippa was obliged to listen to an exhaustive list of all the dainties that they had enjoyed, but noticed with private amusement that both did ample justice to raspberries and cream and freshly made blackcurrant pie. Dr. Merchiston, happily convinced that *his* wise counsel was responsible for this pleasant reconciliation, produced a hoarded Stilton cheese and a bottle of the Marquess's own port. So amiable was his mood that even Dickon was admitted to the masculine coterie for the enjoyment of these delicacies, and bore his part manfully, though Pippa suspected that the sweets were more to his taste. She herself was in the happiest mood, all the miserable heart-searchings of the past six months forgotten. Never mind what the future might bring. The present was bright and comfortable. They even discussed one or two plans for the remaining weeks of the holiday. Nothing was definitely decided, though one or two delightful possibilities were mooted. It was agreed that Dickon, who rode over to Merland most days, could carry messages as regards convenient dates and engagements that could not be evaded.

"With due regard of course, for the overriding importance of the fruit picking season," pronounced Doctor Merchiston solemnly. Pippa giggled.

# Five

Several halcyon days followed. The house party at Merland was gradually dispersing, but Pippa joined them on one of their excursions, having first ascertained from Dickon that Lady Merland had removed for the summer months to Brighthelmstone, a seaside resort which had become very popular with the fashionable since it had won the approval of the Prince of Wales. She spent a delightful day, finding no difficulty at all in meeting so many strangers, and striking up quite a promising acquaintance with one of Quentin's cousins, a young woman of about her own age who was married to an officer in the Navy, and who was beguiling the weary months of his absence by playing hostess for the younger members of the party. Once or twice she rode with her new friends—and their host—and twice, as his guests gradually departed for their own homes, his lordship rode over to sup with the Merchistons.

It was all very pleasant. Pippa, striving to keep a hold on common sense, reminded herself at least twice a day of Lady Merland's cynical remark about marquesses and village maidens. She did not, she assured herself, dream of anything so impossible as marriage. It was just that his lordship had the happy knack of making her laugh; of provoking her to argument; of discussing just those topics that appealed to her sympathies. And perhaps most important of all, of making her feel that she was sweet, loveable if occasionally laughable, and definitely rather special. Someone to be cherished, though without the least fuss or obvious demonstration. Why should she not enjoy his society to the full, since it was all innocent fun and perfectly open? They were never alone together, nor was his attitude in the least flirtatious. If, secretly, she knew that this happy comradeship could not for long endure, she promptly banished the shadow of the desolation that would come with its ending, determined to squeeze the utmost out of each speeding hour.

All too soon it was time for Lucinda to go back to school. She went reluctantly, already planning the festivities that they might enjoy at Christmas. With equal reluctance Dickon set out for his last ride on the bay, Tidewater, to bid his farewells and render his thanks. Quentin had engaged himself to drive the boy home in his curricle and give him one or two hints on the handling of a spirited pair, in an attempt at diverting his thoughts from his impending departure. But when the sound of wheels drew an expectant Pippa to the window, there was no sign of his lordship. One of the Merland grooms was driving, and Pippa got her first inkling that there was something amiss when, having deposited Dickon at the front door, he turned the vehicle and set off at once on his return journey without pausing either to rest the horses or refresh himself. She hurried downstairs to meet a sober-faced Dickon.

His lordship had been called away. He was leaving immediately for Town to make arrangements for a journey to France. Urgent family business. He sent his farewells to Pippa and to Dr. Merchiston, together with his apologies for their unceremonious haste, and would hope to visit them when he returned, but it was impossible to forecast just when this would be.

"To France?" said Pippa, half whispering. For the past three years the name of that fair country had brought unease to simple folk. There were dark tales of cruelty and treachery, of an oppression too great to be born, of the power of the Paris mob. Pippa had heard many such, and understood perhaps a half, swayed first this way by the reported sufferings of the peasants, then the other by the pitiful plight of the emigrés, some of whom she had seen for herself. She had been humbly, if rather ashamedly, thankful that no one she loved was involved in the danger that seemed to threaten every one, whether Royalist or Republican. Why! It was rumoured that even the king and queen were practically prisoners—might possibly be brought to trial. And it was to this land, fraught with lurking, half-comprehended danger, that her beloved was going. The truth was out now. At the thought of injury—captivity—even, perhaps, his death, she sickened and turned cold. What use to pretend any longer that she did not love him? There was even a degree of comfort in the frank acknowledgement. Now she could freely spend all the time she liked in recalling every turn of his head, every inflection of his voice. She could con a treasure house of memory without shame or false pride. And since it was all she would have of him, why not?

Dickon went back to school and she shouldered her burden of anxiety alone. Uncle Philip had listened to the tale of his lordship's departure with a sober face; had occasionally reported scraps of news from France, most of them two or three weeks old. But in general he seemed to feel that the marquess was perfectly capable of managing his own affairs and did not express any undue anxiety. Even when the news of the September massacres reached them, he remained calm. As usual the tales were vague and garbled, but there seemed to be little doubt that in Paris, at any rate, the mob was in command. The deaths of helpless prisoners were reported to number anything up to ten thousand. That, he pointed out, *must* be a gross exaggeration. The prisons could not have held a half of that number. Nor was there any reason to suppose that his lordship was a prisoner, or, indeed, in Paris at all. He had said France, not specifically Paris.

Pippa listened and agreed, but not all the doctor's reassurances could allay the gnawing anxiety that possessed her. And as the weeks went by with never a hint of his return, her conviction grew that some grave mishap had befallen him. A chance encounter with Sir James Waveney did nothing to cheer her. That gentleman couldn't understand what was keeping Quentin in foreign parts when hunting would soon be in full swing.

"Never knew him fail before," he muttered gloomily.

So Pippa slept badly, a prey to frightening dreams, and passed her days in restless, fevered activity. Presently, however, she had cause for more immediate anxiety. Uncle Philip, never one to cosset himself for minor ailments, refused to allow a heavy cold to prevent him from visiting his patients and was caught in a sudden downpour. Soaked to the skin he held on his way and arrived home at dusk chilled and shivering. Next day he was obliged to keep to his bed, and by evening he was in a high fever. Pippa forgot her imagined fears in the need to tend a very sick man.

He was not a demanding patient so much as an awkward one. Understanding the progress of his illness far better than his nurses, he refused at first to have another doctor called in, saying that he knew perfectly well what should be done. Nor would he agree to the attendance of a night nurse, saying irritably that such a one would be sure to wake him just as he had dropped off, wishing him to take his medicine or a cooling drink. But as his fever mounted he grew light-headed, insisting that he must go to his study to find some drug that Pippa had been unable to discover on the shelves and struggling out of bed to do so as soon as he was left alone. Weaker than he had realised, he fell, stunned himself, and lay unconscious on the study floor until found by the anxious searchers. Stubbs was summoned to help him back to bed and it was discovered that in his fall he had also broken his leg. There could no longer be any question of not calling another doctor, and a boy was sent off at once for Doctor Mallow. The two doctors were in fact good friends, enjoying a game of chess when opportunity offered and debating, with far more heat, the comparative merits of the hospitals in which they had studied and such well-known figures in the world of medicine as they had chanced to meet.

Dr. Mallow was cheerful and matter-of-fact. He set the broken bone without much ado, seizing the opportunity to point out to the patient that he was fortunate in being attended by one who had studied under the great Percival Pott. This pleasantry evoked a pallid grin from Dr. Merchiston who, as a loyal Scot, had always upheld the greater prestige of the Hunter brothers.

"And that should stop you from leaving your bed and wandering about where you'd no business to be," announced his friend, adjusting the last bandage. "I'll look in on you tomorrow."

But downstairs in the library he made no secret of his concern. "It's not the leg," he told Pippa. "A clean break, and will do well enough with time. But I don't like his colour or his breathing. Inflammation of the lungs if I'm not mistaken, which I hope I am. Keep him propped up with plenty of pillows to help the breathing. I mean to look at him again tonight. Have to think of some excuse. That's if he's conscious. But I must warn you, my dear, I don't expect it."

He added a few instructions about diet, and left her to her heavy task.

It was heart-breaking. When he was sensible, Uncle Philip was so *good*. He accepted all that was done for him with gratitude; swallowed the draughts that his friend mixed with the shadow of his old quizzical smile, and once with a murmured, "Bone-setter!" which heartened both doctor and nurse considerably. And day by day he weakened visibly and the sound of his painful breathing tore at Philippa's heart. Once or twice, in the occasional lucid interval, he tried to talk to her, but the effort made him cough and soon exhausted him.

On one occasion, when the doctor was with them, he murmured something about his affairs being in order. "I've left the children in your care." His eyes sought Pippa's. "You're young, but you're sensible. And Horace, here is joined with you as guardian. The lawyers will see to the money. I've tied up Richard's share so that he can't fritter it away on buying a commission. A commission. A license to kill. But I don't know. Maybe it would have been better if"—He choked and began to cough, and when the spasm ended, lapsed into silence.

Pippa was so startled by hearing him refer to his son by his baptismal name that for a moment the full import of his remarks did not strike home. Then she said sorrowfully, "He thinks he is going to die, doesn't he? And is fretting over me and the children. He must know that I would not desert them."

Dr. Mallow held open the library door for her. "Of course he does. And it is his greatest comfort," he returned stoutly. He studied the grave, weary little face. "The time has come to be open with you, my child," he said kindly. "You heard Philip say that I was joined with you as guardian. That was all settled between us some time ago. He said then that he did not expect to make old bones, nor, indeed, particularly wish to do so. I very much fear that he was right, and that you must resign yourself to the probability of his death. It is asking a great deal of one so young, but you will do more good by accepting this and by allowing him to talk of his wishes and plans for his family when he is able to do so than by buoying him up with false hopes of recovery. Remember that he knows far better than you do how unlikely that recovery is."

It took a great deal of fortitude to accept so stern a judgement, but Pippa knew that Uncle Philip would have endorsed every word. She took to spending all her time in the sick room, snatching what rest she could in a chair before the fire, and it was the measure of Uncle Philip's weakness that he did not immediately order her out for fresh air and exercise and insist that she had adequate rest. She listened, and answered with hard-held self control when he was sufficiently clear-headed to speak of the dispositions that he wished to make. Once she thought his mind was wandering. She had been brushing out her hair and braiding it for the night, and glanced up to see him watching her.

"Marion," he said slowly. For a moment she thought that he was confusing her with his wife. But as he drew further out of the mists of semi-consciousness he went on, "Marion will scold me. If she had lived she'd have brought you out in proper style instead of letting you waste your youth in this isolated spot. I have been thoughtless and selfish. But God can amend all," and drifted off to sleep again before she could reply.

He had only one more lucid interval after that, and by then the whole household knew that his time was short. He used most of his remaining strength in insisting that his children should not be brought home for his obsequies. Young folk, he whispered, should not have too early an acquaintance with death. "They cannot see that it is right—and even welcome." And with a last glint of humour, "When her mourning is done, see to it that Lucinda does not suffer as you have done. She was not born to blush unseen."

They were his last coherent words. Two days later he died quietly during the small hours. Pippa would have been hard put to it to name the exact hour of his passing.

Dr. Mallow took over the business of arranging the funeral. Mechanically Pippa did all that he asked, having a room prepared for Uncle Philip's lawyer who would be coming from Cheltenham and must be asked to stay the night, giving orders for the preparation of the cold collation which must be set out for the refreshment of such local people as attended the interment. Dr. Mallow warned that there would probably be quite a number as her uncle had been well liked and much respected. But he and Mr. Jarvis, the lawyer, would see to everything. All she had to do was order sufficient food. No one would expect her to preside over the gathering.

She was only too thankful to leave everything in his competent hands. The dull lethargy that had possessed her since Uncle Philip's death seemed to have rendered her incapable of thinking for herself.

But she could not lean on other people for ever. Dr. Mallow had his own work to do, and though he begrudged no effort that might smooth her path there was really very little that could help. He assured her that he and his wife would be very happy to welcome her into their home for a week or two, but when she thanked him but declined, feeling that she was in no mood for constant company, however kind, he did not press the invitation. Perhaps she would prefer to come to them after Christmas, he suggested, when her cousins went back to school. Meanwhile he advised her to get out of doors whenever the weather permitted, to drink a glass of porter with her dinner and to try the beneficial effect of early bedtimes. If she was agreeable, he would do himself the honour of driving over next Sunday to escort her to church. Greeting one's friends and neighbours on such a sad occasion could be something of an ordeal.

Mr. Jarvis explained to her the main provisions of her uncle's Will. There was little of personal concern to her, though she was touched to learn that one or two pieces of Aunt Marion's jewellery had been set aside for her, together with a work-box—a beautiful piece of marquetry work in which she and her aunt had both delighted. She was also to receive a generous allowance until such time as she married, which was kind if not strictly necessary. For the expenses of the household she was to draw upon him, explained Mr. Jarvis. He would examine the books monthly and settle the bills for her. Even in her present state of apathy, Pippa found a little smile for that. A Scotsman to the last. Generous to a fault when it was a question of giving, but still careful over daily expenditure.

The lawyer went on to the management of Dickon's affairs. Pippa had wondered a good deal about this since her uncle's half-disclosure, and it proved to be quite as awkward as she had feared. Her cousin would not inherit fully until he was twenty five. So long as he pursued a course of study leading up to the practice of medicine there was ample allowance for all necessary expenses and even for a few follies. But if he abandoned the life of the medical novice, he was reduced to a beggar's allowance, practically dependant on Pippa's charity for necessary food and clothing.

Pippa burned with indignation. As her first completely natural reaction since her bereavement, it did her a great deal of good.

"My uncle spoke of this arrangement during his illness," she said. "I think he regretted that he had been so—so rigid in his provisions."

Mr. Jarvis nodded, not unsympathetically. "But unfortunately we are left with his written instructions," he pointed out, "and it is my duty to see that those are obeyed. As a trustee," he added pacifically, "I am permitted a degree of flexibility in regard to most expenses. But I am very well aware that my client was utterly opposed to his son's ambitions for a military career. Where that is in question I must follow his directions exactly."

Pippa could only respect his integrity.

As a bachelor he could not offer her a hospitality to match Dr. Mallow's. He strongly advised her to engage a companion, some pleasant genteel female who would be a comfort to her, and to whom she could turn for advice in the difficult task of controlling two lively youngsters. If *he* could be of any service to her in this capacity she must not hesitate to call upon him. She believed him to be sincere and thanked him appropriately, but it was a relief when he finally took his departure and left her alone to brood over the problem of Dickon's future.

# Six

The Christmas holiday was wretched. Dickon and Lucinda, still dazed by their sudden bereavement, were inclined to talk in whispers and creep about the house in a very subdued fashion. Pippa supposed that they grieved for their father in their own way, but they had seen so little of him that his absence did not greatly affect their daily lives. Gradually they reverted to a more normal behaviour, and all too swiftly boredom took the place of low spirits. Pippa could see no reason why they should not entertain their particular friends in a quiet sort of way but there could be no question of noisy parties or of going to see the exciting melodrama produced by the travelling actors or the antics of the performing dogs. Nor were there any horses to ride. And Pippa's promise that this should be remedied as soon as possible could not fill the long dreary days of the present. Moreover it turned the talk to speculation about Lord Merland, which did nothing to raise their spirits, Dickon declaring that everyone said there would be war with France before the new year was out.

And that, of course, brought him to the moment that Pippa had been dreading. Dickon was all for leaving school. He would be seventeen in March, he reminded her. Fellows younger than he were joining the Army. Had Pippa any notion what it would cost to buy a commission in the Artillery? Perhaps he had better consult Doctor Mallow on that head. No doubt it would take some time to arrange, so had best be put in hand as soon as possible. If only Quentin had been available! He would have been just the fellow to advise them as to how best to hurry matters along; perhaps even to have put in a judicious word in the right quarters.

Pippa quailed. For a moment she almost took the coward's way out and left it to Doctor Mallow to tell him the truth. But that would be very unfair, and might lead him to resent the doctor's authority when it came to other matters. She could have wished that Lucinda had not been present, but there was no help for that. Haltingly she explained why Dickon's plan was impossible. He did not rage and storm as she had expected. He went very white, and there was an oddly mature look about the set of the boyish lips, but he heard her out in silence and only nodded thoughtfully when she came to an end. It was almost as though he had expected something of the sort. It was Cindy who broke into tempestuous argument, vowing that if Dickon was not permitted to spend his own money as he wished, *she* would buy him a commission with hers.

Dickon smiled at her in a blind sort of way, murmured something that might have been an expression of gratitude, and went quietly out of the room.

For the rest of the holiday he was very reticent, but he made no further mention of leaving school. Cindy, who had begun the holiday by asking if she, too, could abandon her studies and stay at home to be a comfort to Pippa, had also changed her mind. Possibly even school was more attractive than home under present conditions. Pippa could not blame her. She herself was ill at ease. Though it was never mentioned, all three of them knew that she was perfectly well able to put up the money that would make Dickon's dream come true. But how could she go directly against his father's wishes? She took to imagining that they looked at her reproachfully and bade them both farewell with a certain relief.

Nevertheless she missed them sadly, and made up her mind that something really must be done to make their summer holiday happier. She would write to Sir James Waveney and seek his advice about horses. Those, at least, she could provide without qualms of conscience. And she would have Cindy's room re-decorated.

A modern tent-bed to replace the four-poster would leave room for one or two comfortable chairs and a gate-leg table, so that the child could entertain her friends in a more grown-up fashion and indulge in girlish gossip to her heart's content.

She set about these plans with determined briskness and an aching heart. It was just a year since Dickon had played Samaritan to a certain Quentin Cresswell. For perhaps the thousandth time she wondered where that gentleman was now, and in what case.

She addressed herself to measuring the length for Cindy's new curtains. When they were finished she would start embroidering flannels for Jenny's expected baby. Not that it was expected until the summer, but she must have something to occupy her hands.

There was a tap at the door. Maggie, the young maid who had replaced Jenny, came in to say that there was a gentleman to see her. She sighed. It seemed impossible to get the girl to deal with callers properly. Either she left them standing on the doorstep or she forgot to enquire their names. But she was only fourteen, and a cheerful, willing little soul, decided her mistress indulgently.

At least on this occasion she had shown the gentleman into the library. "Acause 'e cum in a carridge wiv four 'orses," she explained, in support of this decision.

It could only be Sir James, decided Pippa,

and even for him, four horses was a trifle excessive. But perhaps he was on his way to Town. In any case it would not do to keep either him or his horses hanging about while she changed her gown, so she went down to greet him just as she was in the plain grey merino that she had bought as a sop to convention. Uncle Philip had detested all the trappings of grief, grunting something about crape and black bombazine hiding many a thankful heart, but Pippa knew that she was very vulnerable to criticism. She had not yet found a suitable middle-aged female to live with her and did not dare to flout public opinion still further by wearing colours. She would never choose to wear grey or black which made her look insipid and colourless, but what did it matter?

For a moment, as she went in to the library, the clear, February sunlight dazzled her, so that she did not immediately recognise the tall figure outlined against it. Then he turned. She took one hesitant step, scarcely believing that it was really Quentin, and then seemed to spring towards him, both hands outstretched, her pale little face irradiated by joy and thankfulness. And in her delight she forgot such minor matters as proper dignity and a maidenly reserve. Her welcome bubbled out, stumbling and slightly incoherent, but very sweet to a tired and troubled man.

He caught the outstretched hands, drew her

into his arms, and even ventured a light kiss on her cheek as he hugged her warmly and heard her stammered, "M-milord! W-we have been s-so anxious. You cannot imagine how good it is to see you safe and sound once more." And then, realising the impropriety of his embrace, broke free, holding him for a moment at arms' length before she covered her confusion by enquiring with due formality if he would not take some refreshment and then, seeing the weariness in his face, asking in a much more natural way how far he had come and when he had last broken his fast.

"Today?" he said slowly, as though it was difficult to concentrate on speech. "Oh—only from Portishead." And when she cried out at that, saying it must be close on a hundred miles, he added pacifically, "And we stopped at Stroud for coffee. But I was anxious not to spend another night on the road. Denise is asleep in the chaise. Worn out, poor little wretch. And I didn't wake her because I wanted to speak with you alone. I don't quite know how I have the impudence to ask it, but I *do* ask it. Miss Langley, will you take pity on another waif? Will you help me with Denise?"

Miss Langley felt rather as though someone had dashed cold water in her face, but her mood of thankfulness easily surmounted that small shock. She would willingly grant him any support that he needed, and said so.

The tired lines of his face relaxed. "You

blessed child!" he said softly, and without waiting for an invitation dropped into a chair, heaving a great sigh of relief as he stretched weary limbs towards the welcoming blaze. "Though you really should not promise so generously without first enquiring what help is needed," he reproved her, with some attempt at the old, teasing manner.

Pippa studied him thoughtfully for a moment, glanced at the clock and rang for Maggie. It was past three, and it sounded as though he had eaten nothing since breakfast.

"Ask Mrs. Waring to make some sandwiches—beef or ham will do. A mug of ale"—she glanced enquiringly at his lordship, who nodded enthusiastically—"and a plate of Banbury cakes and some tea." He would enjoy the meal better, she guessed, if she made some show of sharing it.

He smiled at her contentedly, that smile that inevitably dissipated the defences that she was for ever erecting against him, so that she turned away hastily and said, almost crossly, "What about—Denise, did you say? And the horses?"

"I'm afraid I left Stubbs to deal with the postilion and the horses," he told her, on a faint note of apology. "As for Denise, perhaps your little maid would keep an eye on her and call us when she begins to rouse. I don't want her to be frightened by finding herself alone."

He did not sound passionately concerned. Just kind. The vague cloud that had threatened

Pippa's new happiness since the mention of the name Denise, receded still further. When Maggie came back with the tray she explained what was required, and the girl bustled off, obviously bursting with mingled importance and curiosity.

When it came to curiosity, her mistress certainly shared it. Who was Denise? How would her coming affect Pippa Langley? She faced what she might hear with courage—but it would not hurt to put off the hearing by insisting that his lordship eat something before he embarked on explanations.

She had her reward. It seemed as though the comfort of the familiar room, the good, plain food, revitalised him even as she watched. When, presently, he replaced the empty tankard on the tray, he smiled at her whimsically and said, "Thank God for English beef and English ale. Do you remember how we talked of foreign lands, and of how much you regretted that your sex made foreign travel practically impossible? I used to feel quite sorry for you. Not any longer! At this moment I feel I would never willingly quit these shores again."

"You have been all this while in France?"

He nodded. "And the tale of my travels will satisfy even Cindy's passion for adventure. But about Denise. Do you think that you could house her and care for her until I can arrange about school or a governess? I know it is asking a great deal, but it would be quite brutal for

98

me to abandon her completely until she has had time to accustom herself to a new way of life. She is beginning to trust *me* and I have talked to her a good deal about you and Dickon and Cindy. I think she could be brought to accept the idea of spending a few weeks with you. She seems to be rather a sickly little creature, but that is hardly surprising after all that she has been through."

Some hostesses might have felt displeasure at the prospect of having a sickly schoolgirl thrust upon them. Pippa, however, began to feel much more kindly disposed towards her unexpected guest.

"You can well understand," his lordship went on frankly, "that I would not dream of taking anything so defenceless to my aunt. My mother would have been the obvious person to take charge of her, but that is what I must explain to you."

Pippa stared. "I did not even know you *had* a mother," she said foolishly.

His lordship was so far recovered that he actually laughed. "It's quite usual, I believe," he suggested, mock apologetic. "I suppose because I haven't chanced to mention her. And I can't imagine why I haven't because I love her dearly. Perhaps the more so because she is not at all the ordinary kind of mother." He hesitated briefly as though picking his words, then went on resolutely, "She is an artist. A good one, too. Not that *that* has anything to say in the matter, except to explain in part why it is an obsession with her. When the painting fit is on she is quite oblivious of other people and their needs. Certainly she would not stop for such ridiculous activities as meals, though failing light does at least oblige her to go to bed at a more or less normal hour. Not the ideal person to have charge of a child who needs cherishing; who needs a steadying routine, a peaceful home and nourishing meals. There is another reason, too, but I will explain that later."

Pippa smiled at him maternally and assured him of her understanding. She wondered what his own childhood had been like, with such an unusual parent.

"I shall hope to make other arrangèments as soon as possible," he promised her. "Meanwhile I would like to put you in possession of the true facts. Denise is my natural sister. I have known of her existence for some years, because my father left me a letter telling me the bare facts and enlisting my support for the child should it ever be needed. Do not be thinking him a heartless rake, will you? I cannot judge between my parents. I daresay there were faults on both sides. I know that Mama would never accompany my father when his diplomatic responsibilities took him abroad. In any case, you and I are not concerned with praise or blame. Papa would have acknowledged Denise and assumed responsibility for her, but her mother would not give her up. Unfortunately the poor lady was killed during street rioting last summer, and her brother wrote asking me to bring Denise away. If you saw the state of affairs in France today—the suspicion, the fear, the senseless violence, you would understand his wish to place her in safety. Unfortunately, before I could do so he had been forced into hiding. I have been all these weeks, first tracking him down—which had to be done without betraying his whereabouts—and then seeking out my poor little sister. But there will be time enough to tell you of our adventures. Sufficient for the moment that we came off safe, and that I have a good friend who is willing to help me out of an uncommonly awkward fix. If it is necessary I will divulge the whole to Mama, though I would prefer not to do so. I leave it to you as to how far you admit your uncle to your confidence."

Pippa started, for the moment completely taken aback. But of course. If he had come straight to her, he could not know of Uncle Philip's death. She herself had grown a little accustomed to her loss and was able to tell him the sad news with a quiet composure that masked her sorrow.

It did not deceive him. "My poor girl," he said slowly, and got up to take her hand in his and press it gently. "If I had known I would not have dreamed of adding to your burdens. Why did you not tell me? I can make some other arrangement for Denise. Perhaps Mrs. Wetherby would take her. I'm afraid I never thought of anyone but you."

Pippa's heart responded happily to the unintentional compliment. "I am glad that you did me so much honour," she told him, "and beg that you will hold by your original plan. Your sister is just what I need. I had not thought to miss Uncle Philip so much. Now that the children are gone back to school I find myself very lonely. Someone to cosset and fuss over is a positive honey-fall. Do tell me more about her. How old is she?"

# *Seven*

Denise had only the clothes in which she had
fled from France. Luckily one or two of Cindy's
outgrown dresses could be made to serve for
the time being, but Pippa felt that an adequate
wardrobe of her own choosing would go far
towards helping her to settle happily into her
new life. For the present she was installed in
Cindy's room because it was next to Pippa's.
She suffered a good deal from bad dreams.
Quentin suggested privily that the sights she
had been obliged to witness both before and
during their escape might easily account for
this. He hoped that fresh surroundings and her
own youthful resilience would gradually efface
the shocking memories. Meanwhile Pippa would
go to her when she woke screaming, and comfort her in nursery fashion, plying her with hot
milk and biscuits and sometimes taking her
into her own bed. Communication between the
two was at first more or less limited to such

practical kindness, since Denise spoke very little English and Pippa's French was of the schoolgirl variety and half forgotten at that.

But timidity was vanquished by the delight of choosing new clothes and Denise's fluency in her new language developed apace by the need to express her views on colour and style, while the first time that she giggled at Pippa's shockingly ungrammatical French marked a significant advance in their relationship.

The resources of the local shops were soon exhausted. Pippa decided that a visit to Cheltenham was necessary. There they could purchase slippers and gloves and the muslins and cambrics that would be needed for summer dresses. She might even buy one or two items for herself, though she was still in mourning. There was to be no thought of crape and bombazine where Denise was concerned. But Cheltenham lay upwards of twenty miles away, and at this season the roads were not good. There were several respectable inns in the town—which enjoyed some fame as an inland watering place—but Pippa was dubious about the propriety of an overnight stay without the chaperonage of an older lady. Quentin solved the problem by lending his travelling chaise for the journey, which might then be accomplished in one day. The plan would have the added advantage of affording plenty of accommodation for all the parcels that they would undoubtedly acquire.

He was a little surprised to find himself wishing that he had gone with them. They would come to no harm in charge of his reliable coachman and groom, and a day spent trailing round shops and warehouses in search of feminine fal-lals was not his idea of a high treat. But he had fallen so much into the habit of riding over to Doctor's Lodge to see how Denise was faring, and then, from one cause or another, of lingering till dusk sent him home, that he found himself quite at a loss as to how to fill in the time. He decided that he ought to pay a duty visit to his aunt, an obligation somewhat overdue. She must have heard of his return by now and would certainly take offence if he delayed much longer in calling upon her.

It did not occur to him that she had not only heard of his return but that she also knew a good deal about his movements *since* that return. He was therefore quite puzzled by the nature of his reception. He was shown into the parlour where he found his aunt snugly ensconced by the fire. Her young relative—what was the girl's name—Dora—Flora—anyway, the one she had hoped to foist on to him as a suitable wife—had been reading aloud to her from some ponderous tome which she now laid down with an air of relief. Her ladyship returned his greeting in the coldest of voices and addressed herself to her protegée.

"Would you be so obliging, my dear, as to

step down to the Rectory and ask Mrs. Verney if she would be so kind as to lend me the second volume of these sermons? I daresay a walk in the fresh air will do you good."

Quenten felt quite sorry for the poor girl. The prospect of having to read such dry stuff seemed a heavy price to pay for half an hour's freedom. Politely he held the door for her as she went meekly on her errand. He bore her no ill will, scarcely knew her in fact. His aunt had described her as such a sweet, biddable girl. He would have phrased it differently and could guess very well what her ladyship had been about. With that spiritless little mouse installed as mistress of Merland, the dowager would never have been away from the place.

He acknowledged the girl's curtsey with a bow and a friendly smile and turned back to his aunt. That lady said icily, "Really, Quentin! You are quite impossible! How dare you come calling here when you must have known that Flora would be with me? The child is to make her début this year. Are you determined to ruin her chances? She is such an innocent that she is quite capable of letting slip the fact that she is pretty well acquainted with you."

His lordship stared at her in amazement. "Well here's a new come-out!" he said indignantly. "Was a time, if memory serves me aright, when you'd have liked to see me a dashed sight better acquainted with her. Why am I suddenly become such an outcast that you must invent a ridiculous errand to remove the wench from my contaminating presence?"

"Do you really imagine that your scandalous behaviour has gone unnoticed?" demanded his aunt, on a note of genuine incredulity. "How naive! Permit me to inform you that what may be commonplace in London or Paris is food for delighted speculation in these rural parts. There was talk enough about your liaison with the Langley girl before you went abroad. But when, upon your return, you visit her before you have so much as removed the dust of travel; when you repeat your visits daily—and in the absence of a chaperone; and when, to crown everything, you have actually persuaded the girl to house the French doxy whom you brought home with you, in order, no doubt, that you may visit the pair of them the more conveniently, you can scarcely wonder that our bucolic neighbours are shocked beyond measure. Why! Only yesterday Mrs. Saxton said to me that the place is no better than a—a bagnio."

By a quite admirable exertion of self control, his lordship kept his temper. He said steadily, "If, by the term liaison, you wish to imply that there has been anything of an improper or clandestine nature between Miss Langley and myself, you are mistaken. Liking grew out of gratitude for her kindness, and I would do a great deal to oblige her if the need arose. My first visit after my return was paid in ignorance of Dr. Merchiston's death. I wished to engage Miss Langley's sympathies for a fifteen-year-old orphan—the child whom you so pithily described as a French doxy. She was entrusted to my care by her uncle, an old friend of my father's. Certainly I have visited her frequently, and shall continue to do so until she has grown a little accustomed to English ways and until I have decided whether to place her in a school or to engage a governess for her."

Lady Merland shrugged, and permitted herself a small satyrical smile. "Most commendable," she told him. "But I fear you will find that our neighbours prefer their own more highly coloured version. To disabuse their minds will prove a difficult, if not an impossible task. Meanwhile I must ask that you do not call here for the present. Flora and I plan to remove to Town at the end of the month, so the prohibition should not subject you to any undue hardship."

His lordship bowed. "As you wish," he said indifferently, and took his leave.

Inwardly he was far from indifferent. There had been an air of smug satisfaction about her that gave cause for concern. He suspected that she had done all she could to foster the spread of those unpleasant stories, even if she had not actually started them. And the stories themselves could do untold damage. Never having been obliged, himself, to pay much heed to the dictates of convention, and conscious—if he had given the matter a thought—of his unimpeachable motives, he had taken no account of the scandal-mongers. Now that their existence had been so forcibly brought home to him, he cursed himself for such criminal carelessness.

His chief concern was for Pippa. Denise was too young for the tittle-tattle to harm her. In any event she would soon be seen to be exactly what he had stated. Pippa was in very different case. Her life might have been unexciting but she had always held the liking and respect of her acquaintance. Her family made no pretensions of grandeur but they could hold up their heads with the best. Was he, who owed her so much, to be the one to rob her of her fair reputation?

He settled down to give some serious consideration to the problem. It did not take him long because obviously there was only one thing to be done. He must marry the girl. And he must do it at once. Never mind that she was in mourning. It would have to be a special licence and a private ceremony, before the gossip could spread further and perhaps reach Pippa's own ears. He knew her well enough to guess that if it did she would refuse him out of hand. It never occurred to him that she might refuse him for any other reason. He was too well accustomed to being pursued as a first rate matrimonial prize.

For his own part, the more he thought of the scheme the better he liked it. To start with, he liked Pippa. He was not in the least in love with her, of course, but persons in his station very rarely were in love with their partners. Nor was she enchantingly pretty—and he had always had an eye for a pretty face. But he was really very fond of her. He liked her better than any other young female that he had met, and if she was not the fashionable heiress of high degree whom he had vaguely pictured as his bride, at least she came of good family and her manners would not put him to the blush. Moreover, unlike many of the charming little barques of frailty with whom he had occasionally dallied in his salad days, she never bored him. Perhaps because she was quite unsophisticated. Her enjoyment of the simplest treat was infectious. And after all, he had always planned to marry some day. Most of his contemporaries had already taken the fatal step, but despite all the lures that had been cast for him he had never seen a girl who was precisely what he wanted. Pippa would do very well.

But despite this complacent attitude he was genuinely concerned to carry the business through with both tact and speed. He understood vaguely that females set a good deal of store on romantic gestures and impassioned avowals of devotion. But the only time that he had sent Pippa flowers she had not been favourably impressed, and she had too much good sense to be taken in by a sudden announcement that he had discovered that he could no longer live without her and that she must marry him at once if she did not wish him to put a period to his existence. Despite the serious nature of his reflections he could not forbear a grin for *that* flight. Knowing his Pippa, she would be more likely to send for a doctor!

He finally decided to make a straightforward approach. Not precisely business-like, but stressing the advantages to both of them if they joined forces. A suggestion that a private ceremony would avoid the restrictions imposed by her mourning, coupled with a hint that both Denise and Dickon would benefit by the arrangement, and a firm assurance of his sincere regard, should turn the trick. Remembering how eagerly she had welcomed him home he felt that he could count on her liking and he did not think that she would hold out against his persuasions. Or perhaps just long enough to preserve dignity and maiden modesty. Better not to drive over tonight, though. Apart from being rather late from a conventional point of view, the young ladies would be newly returned from their shopping expedition and still gloating over their purchases.

Having made up his mind, he was impatient now to have the matter settled. He was off betimes next morning. A sunny spring day seemed to augur well for his purpose and tempted him to ride rather than drive. He clattered into the stable yard at Doctor's Lodge just after ten, an early visitor even by country standards. Since he was riding Ragamuffin there was a brief delay while Stubbs pointed out, with proprietary pride, the animal's complete recovery and total absence of scars. The civilities thus observed, Quentin strode up to the house, his impatience enhanced by the slight check.

He found Pippa engaged in the tedious task of making up the monthly books, an occupation which possibly accounted for her delighted greeting. The sound of scales, painstakingly performed, accounted for the absence of Denise. But when Pippa suggested that she would send Maggie to summon the child, and added, with a chuckle, that she was sure Denise would be only too delighted to abandon her practising, he returned a firm negative.

"Very thankful to find you alone," he said tersely. "Something I wanted to say to you."

Where had they gone? All those easy, graceful phrases that had sprung so naturally to mind last night.

Pippa regarded him with attentive interest. "About Denise?" she suggested helpfully, when he remained silent.

"No. About you. Us," he said desperately. "The thing is—Miss Langley—Pippa—will you marry me?"

For just a moment she stared at him in blank disbelief. Then something in the embarrassment writ plain in his expression convinced her of his honesty. Her own face lit with a radiance

112

that made him feel both humble and uneasy. She held out her hands and said simply, "Yes please."

He heaved a thankful sigh, took the extended hands in his and kissed them, then drew her gently into his arms and lightly kissed her cheek.

Pippa, who had expected something a little more enthusiastic than his chaste salute, smiled up at him with confiding sweetness, but it seemed that his lordship did not mean to let his emotions run away with him.

"I might have guessed that you would give me an honest answer and not keep me dangling in uncertainty," he told her cheerfully. "And now that *that* is settled, I am in hopes that you will consent to my next suggestion. Rather an outrageous one I fear, but if you will hear me out I trust that I can convince you of its desirability. Will you marry me at once, as soon as it can be arranged?"

Pippa was in a mood to agree to anything that he suggested, but already instinct was suggesting that here was some inconsistency. Surely such urgency could only be justified if the gentleman was far more deep in love than his temperate embrace indicated. Instead of the eager consent for which he had half hoped, she hesitated, drew herself out of his casual hold, and awaited further explanation with that air of gentle reserve that was so characteristic.

Quentin began his exposition quite fluently,

but somehow his arguments did not sound so convincing when addressed to that grave, listening face. By the time he came to the end he was shame-faced and stumbling, his usual careless poise in flinders, and the moment did not seem ripe for reassurances about his own feelings.

She did not answer immediately. When she did, there was an unusual note of formality in her voice. "Since I have accepted your very obliging offer, milord, it must be an object with me to meet your wishes so far as my conscience permits. What you have said about Denise and Dickon is all very true, but it does not seem to me to be adequate reason for such intemperate haste." She ventured a little smile. "Marriage is a serious business and lasts a long time. Would you not like to consider its implications more fully? If you wish, we will agree to forget all that has passed between us this morning." He would never know how hard it was to make that offer, but she was glad that she had made it.

His lordship might not be very adept at deceiving a girl for her own good, but he was swift enough to perceive the opening she had given him.

"You have just furnished me with a much stronger reason for pushing on the wedding," he told her, with that disarming smile. "I am not so generous as you. Having once won your consent I have no intention of giving you time

114

for second thoughts. I beg you to agree to my first suggestion and let us be married without delay."

What was a girl to do? Inexperienced as she was, she still sensed that things were not quite as they should be, but in the face of that plea, of the sincerity in face and voice, she yielded.

# *Eight*

During the week that followed, her doubts increased. She was much too sensible to ascribe his lordship's restraint to a chivalrous concern for her unprotected state. If he had really wished to kiss her, she thought, he would certainly have done so. As it was, his behaviour became more and more fraternal. He still came each day to visit them, but the visits were brief and Denise was usually with them. His lordship showed no sign of wishing to be private with his betrothed wife.

There were a good many arrangements to be discussed. Dickon and Cindy would naturally take up residence at Merland during their holidays, and Pippa guessed that they would be very happy to do so. Doctor's Lodge could be left in the capable hands of Mrs. Waring until such time as Dickon was of age to want an establishment of his own.

With some regret they decided against a wed-

117

ding journey. "I would dearly have loved to take you into France and Italy," said Quentin. "So many things that I want to show you. But we shall have to wait until the times are more settled. But we can open up the Town house and I shall enjoy introducing you to London. There is much of interest and of beauty to be explored—and then there are the shops and theatres and concerts. I daresay we shall contrive to pass the time pleasantly enough."

He was everything that was kind and generous and thoughtful. But he did not behave like a man so deep in love that he could not endure to wait more than a week to claim his bride.

A talk with the Rector and his wife did something to calm and support her. Mr. Verney said that it was a pity that her mourning state precluded the gathering of friends and well-wishers to see her married, but added that he would be very happy to know her safe in the keeping of one so well able to protect her and to share the burden of responsibility for her cousins. He did not appear to find anything distasteful in the haste and secrecy with which the wedding was being arranged, even remarking that he had a good deal of sympathy with the marquess's views. Mrs. Verney supported her husband. Woman-like, she regretted that a fashionable wedding with pretty dresses and flowers and music was out of the question, but thought that there was something

118

particularly beautiful and sacred in the small private ceremony that had been agreed.

"And though I know that you would not care for such things, you will be making a marriage of the first consequence. And his lordship so personable and pleasant, with not the least height in his manner. Your uncle liked him, I know, which must be a satisfaction to you, and your dear aunt would have been so happy for you. As we are, my dear. So much as you have been alone—but that will all be mended now."

"And none too soon," she told her husband in the privacy of their carriage as they drove home. "That poor child! If she caught so much as a whisper of the stories that are being put about, she would never hold up her head again. I shall be truly thankful when the knot is safely tied."

Her husband nodded, regretfully. "A very distasteful side of human nature," he agreed. And then, with a mild twinkle, "Of *feminine* human nature, at least."

"With Lady Merland the chief offender," snorted his wife. "Well—this marriage will cut her claws nicely, and very pleased I shall be to see it. It will do her a great deal of good to have to take second place to the new Lady Merland."

Mr. Verney shook his head as in duty bound over this unchristian attitude, but was obliged to admit that his wife had some justification.

"Though his lordship himself admits that he was gravely at fault," he reminded her. "He is going his best to make amends, but he was extremely thoughtless and careless."

Mrs. Verney had a soft spot for his lordship. "He is still young," she said indulgently. "He *meant* no harm—which is more than can be said of his lady aunt. And he seems to hold Philippa in some affection." She hesitated a moment, then said slowly, "Do you think it will be a successful marriage? For though Pippa is a dear girl, she is quite unused to Society. I daresay she will learn quickly, for she is intelligent, but I hope that her husband will be patient and sympathetic when she makes mistakes."

"She is not only intelligent," corrected her spouse. "She is a girl of well-established character, with a strong sense of duty and a good deal of kindly humour. His lordship does very well for himself. And I believe him to be sincerely attached to her—perhaps more deeply than he realises. I should not otherwise have given countenance to the match, nor accepted the plea for strict secrecy. It is fortunate that Philippa's recent bereavement can be made to serve as sufficient reason for *that*. Otherwise it would certainly give rise to even more unpleasant tittle-tattle, and quite defeat his lordship's intention."

His wife allowed herself to be soothed by his

firm pronouncement and went on to speak of other matters.

Philippa was not quite so deaf and blind as her good friends hopefully supposed. Though blessedly ignorant of the main reason for the hurried and secretive marriage, she was wide awake on other suits. In the few days that had been granted her for reflection she had come to realise more and more certainly that her promised husband did not love her as she longed to be loved. She had faced the fact with as much honesty as might be expected of a deeply interested party, and had decided to marry him just the same. An unlooked-for opportunity had been tossed at her feet, and she would make the most of it. No thought of rank or wealth tarnished this single-minded purpose, and if, once or twice, her courage faltered, she reminded herself of Uncle Philip's advice. She would *not* choke herself on pride! If the conditions of her new life were not wholly to her liking, she would still accept them humbly, gratefully, and make what she could of them. Perhaps—she had read that sometimes it was so—closer acquaintance would serve to turn mild affection into something deeper and warmer. Certainly no effort of hers should be spared to achieve this desirable end. Resolutely she closed her eyes to the desolation that the future might hold. It was a poor spirit that counted the cost of disaster before the campaign was even launched.

Meanwhile she schooled herself to match Quentin's undemonstrative attitude, careful to conceal the surge of vivid happiness that his very presence brought, turning a cool cheek to receive his kiss.

Two days later they were married.

Mrs. Verney and Dr. Mallow served as witnesses. Dr. Mallow also gave the bride away. He was in no sense her guardian, but as Uncle Philip's friend she had naturally turned to him. Quentin had approved the choice and had himself explained the circumstances to the doctor, earning thereby a grunt of approval and a shrewd glance from beneath shaggy brows which indicated that some sort of rumour had already reached their owner. There had been little time to think about a wedding dress, but Pippa, who did not want to wear mourning on her wedding day, had hastily altered a scarce-worn dress of Aunt Marion's. It was old fashioned of course, but the material was charming, a soft silk, the colour of mother-of-pearl, that glowed with delicate rainbow hues as the wearer moved. She carried a tight little posy of pink tulips that had been sent over from Merland very early, together with a note from the bridegroom. The note contained no protestations of undying devotion, merely a teasing reference to another occasion on which he had sent her flowers and a hope that this time she would accept them more graciously, but it did a good deal for Pippa's spirits. It sent her up the aisle on Dr. Mallow's arm with a shy radiance in her face, and she made her responses quietly but steadily. If most of the tiny congregation heaved secret sighs of relief when at last the knot was fairly tied, the bride, after one enquiring glance at her new husband, seemed more concerned with the nice arrangement of the flowers that Mrs. Verney had just restored to her.

It had been settled that they should return to Doctor's Lodge after the ceremony to partake of a cold collation and to drink a toast to the married pair. Dr. Mallow apologised for a premature departure from the gathering, pleading pressure of work, and the Verneys did not linger unduly after his going. Mrs. Verney kissed Pippa's cheek, assuring her that she looked quite delightfully and repeating good wishes for a long and happy married life. "Milady," she concluded quizzically.

Pippa flushed scarlet and choked on a sip of wine. Quentin shook his head at the speaker.

"And I had been *so* careful not to draw her attention to that aspect of her new state," he said lightly. "Don't let it oppress you, my love. You will soon become accustomed. After a month or so I daresay you will realise almost at once that people mean *you* when they address you so."

The Verneys laughed, and went out on a wave of good humour, something of their concern for the success of this unusual marriage a little allayed.

Pippa turned to her husband, still composed, though her voice was taut as she said, "You do not imagine that I consented to marry you because of *that*?"

It was his cue to take her in his arms and vow that, whatever her reason, he would not quarrel with it since it had given him his heart's desire. Instead he said kindly, "Of course not! You married me because we go on so comfortably that we would like to travel the rest of the way together."

That was good honest truth; and, for his lordship, the phrasing was almost poetic. To Pippa it was like being offered a stone when she hungered desperately for bread. In a colourless little voice she said, "So long as you acquit me of venal motives," and thought she had best enquire if Denise had finished packing.

It was only the presence of Denise that prevented the strain of the day from becoming unbearable. Her eager chatter beguiled the journey to Merland, and the comical mistakes in her mixture of French and English provoked one or two unfeigned chuckles from the sedate bride.

She accompanied them on a tour of the great house. "Rather more extensive than the one we provide on Public Days," explained Quentin with a reminiscent gleam.

Pippa was so absorbed in this first intimate inspection of the rooms that she would occupy as Quentin's wife that for a little while she forgot her sore heart and behaved much more naturally. Despite the elegance of the furnishings she decided privately that there was scope for improvement. Merland had been without a mistress for some time. Nor was the dowager, she judged, a home maker. There was a chilly formality about the reception rooms despite the perfection of their appointments, and the smaller rooms set aside for the use of the lady of the house were stiff and uninteresting. Probably they had been little used. Pippa could well imagine that domestic cosiness would be little to the dowager's liking. She began to consider which of her own possessions should be brought to Merland and to discuss the refurnishing of the schoolroom for Denise and Cindy. Apart from one or two awkward moments when Denise displayed an embarrassing interest in the allocation of the bedchambers and vowed that she would be afraid to sleep alone in the vast four-poster that was considered appropriate to the dignity of the lady of the house, the afternoon passed pleasantly enough.

But changing her gown for dinner in the cold magnificence of the vast room, Pippa began to dread the moment when Denise would go off to bed and leave the two of them alone. It was all so different from what she had expected. In her intense preoccupation with the personal side of her marriage, she had forgotten that there would be a public side, too. For the first time she knew doubts about her own adequacy. Her campaign to win her husband's love must be fought out on this unfamiliar ground. To be making foolish mistakes would scarcely serve to endear her to him, and while he had never seemed to care much for his own consequence he would certainly expect his wife to comport herself with a dignity suited to the high rank that he had bestowed upon her. She sighed as she slipped her wedding gown over her head. Wearing it was a gesture of defiance. Perhaps she should have yielded to convention and resumed her mourning. But the dress buttoned down the front which had enabled her to decline the services of a maid, and it was more becoming than anything else that she possessed. Tomorrow she would be docile and obedient. She would begin to plan a new wardrobe—which was a pleasant thought—and draft an advertisement for the services of a lady's maid—which was not. Tonight, for her first dinner at home with her husband, she would wear Aunt Marion's pretty silk. She brushed her hair until it shone, coiled it smoothly round her head, and braced herself to face the ordeal of a formal dinner with fortitude.

But it was not an ordeal after all. Certainly it was a festive meal. A flurried housekeeper had done her best to dignify the occasion despite short notice. The food was delicious, though many of the dishes were unrecognisable by Pippa's simpler standards. There was an array of creams and jellies that caused Denise to clasp her hands ecstatically, and his lordship insisted that both ladies take wine with him. He had also had the good sense to have the meal served on the small table in front of the library fire. He was in the habit, he explained, of using this in preference to the enormous one in the dining room which, when fully extended, would seat sixty.

"I have no great liking for formality," he added, "though you, my dear, must do exactly as you choose, and there are, of course, occasions when it is essential."

Somewhat heartened by these remarks, and possibly even more so by two glasses of the cool, bubbling champagne that her husband himself poured for her, Pippa enjoyed her dinner. Once the first course had been removed his lordship dismissed the servants, and without the constraint of their presence, talk became more animated. There had been so little time to make plans together that Quentin had been obliged to make several tentative arrangements for which he now sought approval. Would Pippa like to go up to Town at the end of the week? He had given orders for Merland House to be made ready to receive its new mistress and for extra servants to be engaged. "There will be a great deal to do," he told her. "You must be presented, you know, upon your marriage. Which means your Court dress to be ordered without loss of time. Then you will be wanting to buy a great many clothes and will need to hire a dresser to look after them for you. But most of all, of course, I want you to meet my mother."

He sounded so calm and matter-of-fact that Town life, a Court dress, even her presentation, seemed natural and inevitable. Meeting his mother was something different again. *That* she reserved for later consideration.

Meanwhile she said thoughtfully, "And Denise?"

Here, too, his lordship had made provision. He had written to his Cousin Claudia—the one who was married to a naval officer and with whom Pippa had struck up a friendship— asking if she would like to spend the summer months at Merland and give an eye to Denise. He shot that young lady a wary glance, wondering how far her English had progressed, and added swiftly in an undervoice, "She is increasing, you see—Claudia—and cannot go about in Society. I think she will be happy to oblige us, and it will be more cheerful for her than a hired house in Portsmouth with no one of her own family to bear her company. Here she has a number of friends—and *we* shall be backward and forward a good deal. Moreover it will save her a good deal of expense—and Perry has very little beyond his pay."

Pippa had never realised that there could be straitened means in such exalted circles, or that such a one as her husband, himself one of fortune's favourites, would give a thought to them. She heartily approved the scheme, and between discussing which rooms would be most suitable for Claudia's use and considering the kind of carriage that she herself would drive and how many horses she would need, she was soon quite at ease. She had ridden very little of late years and had never driven anything more exciting than a gig, but at least this prospect caused her no trepidation. It lay within the realms of the familiar.

Denise grew sleepy from mingled excitement, strange food and champagne, and went off yawning to the schoolroom wing, leaving her elders happily engrossed in arranging a programme for Pippa's first visit to the Metropolis. At first it appeared that there was a considerable divergence of taste between them, but Pippa's schoolgirl notions soon yielded to her husband's more sophisticated views. He allowed that the Tower of London might be worth a visit, as might Westminster Abbey and St. Paul's Cathedral, but museums were fusty and boring. Vauxhall Gardens, of which Aunt Marion had spoken wistfully, were slightly out of fashion. Ranelagh was all the crack. And though it was far from fashionable, he rather thought she would enjoy Astley's Circus. Theatres and concerts, of course, and even the Opera could be quite amusing. An opinion which considerably surprised his naive listener, who had not thought it so intended. It was a pity that she would not be able to dance while she was in mourning, but there was no reason why they should not attend any number of parties and balls as spectators.

Pippa was in the midst of explaining that this was actually a fortunate circumstance, since her dancing would never pass muster in fashionable circles and that she would have to arrange for some lessons, when the front door bell rang. It was rung with considerable vigour and the ring was followed by a brisk assault upon the door knocker. This visitor was obviously determined upon admittance, and since it was nearly ten o'clock their eyes met in surprise and speculation.

"Someone needing help," surmised Quentin. "Urgently, too. House on fire, or a carriage accident."

But it was the homely figure of Dr. Mallow that was ushered into the room, and though he appeared harassed and was much put about at being obliged to intrude upon them at so late an hour, his errand was not concerned with such dramatic happenings as Quentin had imagined.

"It's young Dickon," he said abruptly, when he had done apologising. "Run away from school. Left them a letter to say he was off to join the Army, and not to look for him, because if he was taken back he'd only make off again first chance he got."

One of the under masters, a fellow called

Brook, had arrived just as he sat down to his belated dinner. They owed the prompt discovery of the lad's escapade to him, since he had been returning from a private errand when he had caught a glimpse of a familiar-looking figure boarding the London stage. Upon his return to the school he had at once instituted enquiries, and Dickon's note had been discovered. They had sent immediately in pursuit of the stage, but when the messenger caught up with the lumbering vehicle his quarry had already left it, and a cursory search of the fields and farms bordering the road had discovered no trace of him. Mr. Brook, it emerged, was to some extent in the boy's confidence, though not, of course, privy to this foolish prank. At any rate he was well aware of Dickon's military ambitions, and held it to be rather more than a prank.

Pippa, recovered now from the first shock of the news, nodded soberly. "I should have thought of it," she said. "It was not natural that he should have taken his disappointment so quietly. He must have had this in mind for some time."

"Well that's all very well," growled the doctor. "And I'm not saying I don't sympathise with him to some extent. But he can't be permitted to kick over the traces in this reckless fashion. We must find him and get him back. Then we can see what's to be done."

"And perhaps that is where I can help you," put in Quentin quietly. "You cannot be expected to neglect your other responsibilities to go hunting for one pesky boy. If you will entrust the task to me, I will do my possible. Though I am not his guardian we get on pretty well together and his faith in my worldly knowledge is positively alarming. If only I can find him, it should not be too difficult to persuade him to come home—at least until we can discuss his future career more thoroughly. Will they have him back at school if he gives his word not to abscond again?"

For a moment the doctor looked dubious. Then his face brightened. "If your lordship were to go bail for him, I reckon they would," he opined. "Brook says he's a good sort of lad, sensible and well-liked. But he's to be found first of all, and I don't above half like putting the job on you. When all's said and done, it's my responsibility."

"Well I certainly couldn't doctor your patients," returned Quentin cheerfully, "but I'll back myself to track down a runaway schoolboy as well as the next. Suppose we each stick to the job we can do best?" And Dr. Mallow yielded thankfully to this sensible view of the matter.

When he had taken his departure, Quentin turned to his wife. "You will have to forgive me, my dear. A shocking thing to desert you on our wedding night. I can only plead that he is *your* cousin. You will understand that this business brooks no delay. The boy will take no harm if he succeeds in enlisting—though it may be a rough and disillusioning experience. It's the thought of the other dangers that surround him—no more than a guinea or two in his pocket, I daresay, and every rogue and sneak-thief on the look-out for a green 'un—that makes me urgent to be gone. Fortunate that it's full moon. I'll enlist a groom or two—some of Dickon's particular cronies who will be eager to help—and send you news as soon as I have any. Keep up your courage—and forgive my desertion." With which he kissed her soundly, with considerably more determination than he had ever shown before, and went off to change into riding clothes.

His wife was left to wonder whether this sudden display of dominant masculinity was due to the prospect of imminent action or to re-lief at his escape from his matrimonial respon-sibilities.

# Nine

Despite his confident claim it took Quentin three days to track down the runaway, and t vo more to return him to school and persuade the authorities to accept him. In return for a certain promise, Dickon himself was ready to eat humble pie and to accept any punishment that might be meted out to him, but his preceptors were less amenable. It took Quentin's best persuasions, backed by all the weight of his rank and influence, to win their consent, on a solemn undertaking from the culprit to submit himself to school discipline until such time as his new cousin could arrange his entry into the army on more orthodox lines. It was his lordship's plea that expulsion from school would inevitably blast a promising career at the outset that finally turned the trick.

He had sent word to Pippa as soon as he had the boy safe in his keeping, but she had had ample time to imagine a number of unpleasant and dangerous situations in which Dickon might find himself, and not all her common sense could really convince her that most of them were highly improbable.

Had he but known it, her cousin could scarcely have done her a greater service. The great household to which she had come was divided in its attitude towards her. Its younger members thought her marriage was romantic—just like a fairy tale—but there were several doubters. Romsey and Mrs. Hayward, the butler and housekeeper, who had seen many years in Merland service, were two who had reserved judgement. To be sure, they agreed, it was high time that his lordship married, *and* set up his nursery, but was this young lady worthy of the high position to which she had been so suddenly elevated? There was a look of breed about her and she had pleasant unassuming manners. But she was an unknown, with neither rank nor wealth to commend her—so far as they knew. To their credit be it said, both ignored the scandalous stories that they, in common with every other servant on the place, had heard. But that was because they knew his lordship.

"I'm not saying that he hasn't had dealings with the muslin company now and now," pronounced Romsey judicially. "But only with such as well knew what they were about. He'd never meddle with a gently born girl like her young ladyship. And *we* know the Lady Dowager, don't we, now? I'd not seek the source of these wicked tales any further than the Dower House."

Mrs. Hayward nodded sagely. "You don't know what a difference it makes," she confided. "The master being a decent gentleman as well as a noble lord. One place I know of, there's never a maid servant safe from improper advances. And while I'll not pretend there's not some as welcomes them, mothers of decent girls won't let them take service in such a household. What's more, those that do mostly live to rue the day. Like should keep to like," she ended significantly.

"Aye. And there's the rub," nodded Romsey. "We'll just have to wait and see."

Thanks to Master Dickon's cantrips they saw a good deal, and sooner than they had expected. They saw how the newcomer bore herself in adversity. Let alone that it was no small matter to have your bridegroom snatched away on your wedding night, it was plain to the discerning eye that the young lady suffered considerable anxiety over her errant cousin. In a great household there are few secrets. To add to the pale cheeks and shadowed eyes, the swiftly repressed start when the bell rang or a carriage drove up, everyone knew of rumpled sheets that betokened restless nights, and of dishes barely tasted despite the cook's best endeavours. Yet her ladyship never failed in courtesy or composure. She dealt gently with "the little foreign wench's" moods and whims, never forgot to thank either man or maid who performed a service for her, and quite won Mrs. Hayward's heart when that lady offered, with some formality, to hand over the keys which for years had been her badge of office by saying, "Oh, no! Please! I wish you will keep them! It is no light task to keep a house well tended and comfortable, especially one of this size. I took pride in keeping my uncle's house to the best of my ability. I *like* housekeeping and will be very happy to learn of you. But you must know that, setting aside his lordship's fondness for established ways of which I know nothing, I should make a dozen mistakes in half an hour. The more so at this present since I am preoccupied with my cousin's affairs. Pray don't throw me to the wolves, Mrs. Hayward. My whole dependence is on you!"

Which, as the good lady later said to Romsey, couldn't have been spoke more handsome, not if she'd been the Queen herself.

In normal circumstances Pippa might have been diffident, morbidly anxious not to make mistakes in this strange new world, the more so since she had been deprived of Quentin's support. But concern for her cousin put such thoughts out of her mind, and when she discovered that the members of her new household genuinely shared that concern she found it easy to be her natural friendly self. Dickon, having run tame at Merland during his holidays, had earned a considerable degree of liking, and there were many enquiries for the latest news of him. In the seemingly endless days that elapsed before Quentin sent word that he was safe, Merland and its new mistress came to an acceptance of each other that might otherwise have taken months.

Her mind relieved of its most pressing anxiety, she embarked on a more detailed exploration of her new home. But now she met friends everywhere. They were respectful and correct, but their eyes were alive and welcoming. The veiled curiosity of which she had been aware on her wedding day might never have been, and the older servants were so eager to explain their duties and responsibilities, to boast of long service or the importance of their particular place in the hierarchy, that the exploration became a long and leisurely business with frequent deviations into the family histories of the various speakers. Pippa had no idea that she was winning golden opinions. In her quiet life she had often felt lonely and rather useless. Here was a whole world of people who would be partly dependent on her for their contentment and security, who were already beginning to confide in her and tell her their troubles. She reacted to this atmosphere like a parched flower to gentle rain, and listened with absorbed interest to the rambling stories, offering sympathy and occasionally, shyly, a word of practical advice.

She emerged briefly from this welter of domesticity to consult with Mrs. Hayward and the cook on the important subject of choosing a meal fit to set before her returning lord. He would be tired and hungry, and there would be a good deal to talk about. Something tempting and hot, that could be served quickly if the traveller should chance to be delayed, she suggested tentatively. The cook looked slightly affronted at this reflection on his talents. Mrs. Hayward began to suggest dishes, all of which, the pair declared, were prime favourites with the master, until the projected menu began to sound like a royal banquet. She left them debating the respective merits of roast goose and fillet of veal with high sauce, and went off to consult Romsey about wine.

Between his wife and his servants, all united in the desire to make the evening meal a second and even more successful wedding feast, Quentin found the reception that awaited him a little overwhelming. He was very tired, having been in the saddle almost constantly during the early part of his absence with little opportunity to rest since. He had sustained a difficult interview with his new cousin, steering carefully between the tongue lashing prompted by mingled weariness and relief and an expression of sympathy for the boy's single-minded determination. Then there had been the delicate manoeuvring to win over the school authorities. Finally he had been obliged to complete his homeward journey on a hired horse, which proved to be touched in the wind and had to be carefully nursed lest it founder completely. He wanted nothing so much as his bed. But despite the urgent reason for his going, he felt vaguely guilty over the cavalier fashion in which he had deserted his bride, and supposed, yawning, that he had better do the pretty.

It was not difficult. The library fire was comforting and Romsey had opened a bottle of his favourite claret. Champagne, that experienced gentleman had informed his underlings, was very well for ladies, and of course for a ball or a coming of age. But there was nothing like a good smooth claret or a burgundy to please the gentlemen. His lordship, who had eaten nothing since breakfast, was soon in the mood to agree with him. He did not fully appreciate the perfection of the fillet of veal—indeed he could not have said precisely *what* he was eating. But it was hot, savoury and satisfying. And his wife, who had somehow developed a becoming little air of confidence during his absence, had displayed a gratifying appreciation of his efforts on Dickon's behalf. He permitted Romsey to refill his glass, consented to essay the roast goose, and relaxed comfortably. There was something to be said, after all, for the married state. It was really quite pleasant to come home to such a welcome; to have so absorbed a listener hanging on his every word. She had even suggested that he should not trouble to change his dress, since he was so tired. He had naturally pooh-poohed the idea. But the thought *had* just drifted through his mind that it would be rather agreeable to sup informally together when they were not entertaining guests. No servants, casual confortable clothes rather than evening rig, the sort of evening that he used to enjoy with Cherry. Then he recalled that Cherry had been his mistress, not his wife, and hastily dismissed the notion.

He signed to Romsey to replenish his glass and raised it in a formal toast to Pippa. They finished the meal in lazy amity and sat on talking in the candle light, discussing the arrival of Cousin Claudia and the arrangements for their own departure, Quentin confessing that he would be thankful to have a whole day idling at home before being obliged to set out on his travels once more.

"The onset of old age," he told her, grinning, "accelerated, I feel sure, by the heavy responsibilities of matrimony."

She refused to take issue with him on that head and presently bade him good night, leaving him to finish his wine and shyly hoping that it would not be too long before he joined her. She was not afraid of the physical side of marriage. It was just that she did not want to think about it for too long, growing more and more shy and self conscious. At least there was no waiting abigail to add to her embarrassment, she thought gratefuly, as she pulled on her bed gown. It was a demure garment of fine linen, buttoning high to the throat, but it was her best, because there was pretty stitchery gathering the ample folds into the yoke. She began to brush her hair and braid it for the night, the hand that held the brush shaking a little in her nervousness, her breath coming quick and shallow as she listened for any sound that might indicate her husband's coming.

Quentin finished his wine and stood up, stretching luxuriously. Best give her a little longer, he decided. In his experience, women made as much pother over getting ready for bed as they did over dressing for a ball, what with perfume and powder and trailing, transparent negligees. He yawned again, hugely, poured himself some brandy, and settled down in a comfortable chair beside the fire. Ten minutes later he was deeply asleep.

# Ten

It proved surprisingly difficult to put matters right next day. He had wakened in the small hours, chilled and stiff. Pippa must have been asleep hours ago. Certainly there was no light showing under her door. He had undressed quickly and dropped into bed, to fall asleep again almost at once. It was not until next day that it occurred to him that there might be any awkwardness about making his apologies. But the more he thought about it, the more diffi- cult it seemed to put his feelings into words. Had their marriage been a few months old, the small lapse might have passed unnoticed—or at least been regarded as comical. But—last night—she must have been expecting him to come to her. How could he say that he had fallen asleep? Without hurting her feelings?

And the cool, poised little creature who faced him across the breakfast table and politely enquired if he would take tea or coffee, did nothing to help him. Besides, it was too delicate, too intimate a matter to be discussed within the hearing of servants. He decided, with some relief, to await a better opportunity.

It did not arise. After his week's absence there were a number of small matters demanding his attention, and in view of his impending departure they must be dealt with today. His wife, too, proved surprisingly elusive. Instead of hanging on his arm, seeking his advice or permission for her every action, she might have been the châtelaine of Merland for years, going off so calmly to discuss menus with Mrs. Hayward and the cook. He was not sure that he quite liked such competence, though he had to admit that it would have been a dead bore to be obliged to accompany her in all her domestic duties. Nevertheless this independence sorted ill with his mental image of a docile and helpless little wife to whom he would be so very kind and forbearing.

Cousin Claudia was to come to them that day. She was travelling in the care of an uncle and aunt who were on their way to Cheltenham to drink the waters. A fortunate circumstance, she had written, since in her present condition it was thought inadvisable for her to travel with only an abigail for escort. Since she was not expecting to be confined until the end of July, Pippa had been mildly surprised, but it emerged that the poor girl suffered dreadfully from travel sickness at the best of times.

The uncle and aunt had declined an invitation to stay overnight, being anxious to press on to their destination and the relief of Sir Martyn's gout and his wife's dyspepsy. But obviously, for the honour of Merland, they must be persuaded at least to take some refreshment and to see Claudia comfortably settled. When Quentin suggested to his wife that they should stroll in the grounds for half an hour, this visit furnished reason sufficient for her to excuse herself. Her very first visitors, she pointed out. She must be sure that all was in perfect order.

He might have answered that there were servants and to spare to deal with such things, but this morning they were being distantly polite to each other so he merely nodded and turned on his heel. Her lips quivered; almost she called out to him that she would come. But she wanted time to think.

Behind the surface composure lay a seething whirl of conjecture. Why had he not come to her last night? Nothing so simple as the real reason even occurred to her, and most of the others were too humiliating for contemplation. But until she could see her situation rationally and clearly she would make no definite move. Listlessly she busied herself in arranging flowers in Claudia's rooms.

Sir Martyn and his lady proved to be a mild, inoffensive pair, much absorbed in their ailments and the treatments they proposed to take, and therefore very easy to entertain. If they studied Pippa with rather more interest than was strictly courteous, she was unaware of it, being more concerned with Claudia's sickly looks and air of exhaustion. It was obvious that the journey had tried her a good deal, but she did not want to make a fuss and summoned up energy to felicitate her cousin upon his marriage and even to commend the good sense he had shown in making his choice, which, she said, with a pallid little grin, was more than she had expected. Pippa thought she would be better laid upon her bed with a hot brick to her feet instead of cutting foolish jokes, but she respected the determined fortitude and contented herself with seeing that Claudia's tea was poured just to her liking and then leaving her to sip it in peace while she herself deflected the well meaning efforts of Lady Chalfont to persuade the girl to eat.

She was thankful when the Chalfonts took their leave, promising that they would do themselves the honour of calling again on their way home to see how Claudia was going on, and promptly took charge of her friend, insisting that she should rest.

"You didn't bring a dresser, did you? Good. Then I shall wait on you myself and Dimity shall unpack for you later. Now don't argue! Remember that I am almost as good as a doctor—better, sometimes—and do as I say. You shall have a comfortable nap which will make you feel much more the thing, and then presently you and I will have a snug little supper together while you tell me all your news. No, of course Quentin will not mind. Not many gentlemen are permitted to revert to their bachelor freedom after only a week of matrimony. I daresay he will be delighted."

If there was an acid undertone to this remark, Claudia was too exhausted to notice, but it caused Quentin to look very thoughtfully at his wife. He said urbanely, "By all means. I shall ride over and take pot-luck with James. Most convenient, actually. There are one or two matters I want to discuss with him before I go up to Town, and it will be much simpler than writing to him."

He knew very well that his attitude was childish. His conscience was still uneasy about last night and his failure to explain matters to his wife. But if she chose to be pettish she could come home by Weeping Cross.

Nevertheless he was not really surprised when he reached home again after a very dull and remarkably abstemious evening, to find a note from the lady explaining that she had decided to spend the night in Claudia's room. The poor girl had suffered another bout of sickness, and though she was now much recovered it had left her very low-spirited. Very well, submitted his lordship grimly. But tomorrow we shall be in Town, and there will be an end to all this shilly-shallying. If she will not see sense, I shall shake it into her.

They breakfasted very early—and were meticulously polite to one another. Claudia was having breakfast in bed, but was reported to be quite herself again and looking forward to a long, lazy summer. Quentin said that he would look in on her to say goodbye and reminded his wife that it would not do to be lingering. They must be on the road betimes if they meant to reach Town that night. The lady assured him that she would not keep him waiting.

It might have been thought that the long coach journey would afford ample opportunity for the pair to reach understanding. On the surface all was smooth. Pippa was genuinely interested in a countryside which was new to her and in all the activities of the road, and in answering her questions and pointing out various places of interest the time passed pleasantly enough. Yet neither was really at ease. Quentin sought in vain for an opportunity to explain that he had not meant to be neglectful. Whenever there was a pause in the conversation, Pippa made haste to fill it with some comment on the scenery or the performance of the horses, and it would scarcely mend matters to break across her remarks with a total change of subject. Better to wait until he had her safe in Merland House. Meanwhile he devoted himself to ensuring her entertainment and her comfort.

They stopped for coffee in Oxford. It was Pippa's first sight of the ancient city and she was entranced by its beauty. She drank her coffee in a dream, planning the longer visit that she would make some day, and did not at first realise that they were attracting a good deal of attention. But she could scarcely fail to notice the landlord's obsequious bearing when he presented the reckoning, or miss the murmured, "A great honour, milord." No doubt inn servants were swift to recognise wealthy patrons. And now several other people were staring at them with open curiosity. She was suddenly conscious that her appearance was in no way worthy of such notice. Her travelling cloak was neat and warm, but it was two years old. It sorted ill with her husband's careless elegance. She felt her cheeks colour under the appraising stares of the company and bit her lip in exasperation that she should be so easily put out of countenance. Quentin appeared quite unaware of the stir they had caused, and presently handed her up into the carriage with as much care as if she had been a princess of the blood, completely indifferent to the curious, watching eyes.

One could not but like him the better for that. She said slowly, "I fear I do you small credit, milord." And, at his enquiring gaze, indicated the offending cloak.

"Well that is a matter that can easily be mended," he returned lazily. And then, "At least the colour is becoming. It brings out the chestnut glow in your hair."

151

If only he had said that first, thought Pippa wistfully, instead of giving tacit agreement to the suggestion that she did him little credit. She enquired if they were still making good time.

They were. But after Oxford the weather worsened. They ran into heavy rain and the pace dropped. By the time that they plodded into Beaconsfield it was obvious that it would be very late indeed before they reached Town, but when Quentin suggested that they should rack up for the night, Pippa begged to go on. After her experience in Oxford she had no wish to run the gauntlet of curious eyes in yet another inn, though naturally she did not tell her husband this. He was more than a little doubtful as to the wisdom of pressing on, but at least the rain had stopped and the waning moon was no longer obscured by drifting clouds, so she was allowed to have her way.

There had been heavy rain in this part of the country, too, and the road more nearly resembled a quagmire. By the time they reached the paved streets, Pippa was regretting her decision to push on to their destination. She was chilled to the bone despite her warm cloak and the rug that his lordship had tucked about her, her head ached and she felt distinctly queasy.

Fortunately they were expected. His lordship, greeting his butler and his housekeeper in his usual easy style, presented these dignitaries to his wife, took one look at her white face and suggested that she should retire at once. Since it was after midnight she was only too thankful to obey. Mrs. Dunstable bore her off, rather like a ship of the line convoying a frail yacht, murmuring soothing promises about a warm bed and a cup of hot chocolate, "For your ladyship will not be wanting to drink coffee at this late hour," and wondering privately what his lordship had seen in such an insignificant little piece to prompt him to matrimony.

But a night's sleep did much to restore Pippa to her cheerful equable self. She sat up in bed, drinking the tea that a neat housemaid had brought, and surveying the elegance of her room. Last night she had been too weary. Today she looked at it critically and thought that it, too, bore the stamp of the Dowager's personality. A cold perfection, the newly lit fire crackling on the hearth supplying the only homely note. Well—grandeur and formality might be desirable in the reception rooms, but in her own private apartments there would have to be some changes. First, however, there would have to be a great many changes in her own appearance. The abigail who had brought her tea had seemed a pleasant child. She would ask Quentin which shops she should patronise, and the girl could go with her. At once. Until she was more fashionably dressed she was in no mind for sociability.

But Quentin, duly consulted over the breakfast table, had other views. Certainly she must replenish her wardrobe without loss of time, but there was one engagement that could not be delayed.

"I must take you to meet my mother. It is quite bad enough that I should not have done so before we married, though I promise you that she will not hold *you* to blame. But if she learned that we had been in Town above a day without going to see her, she would be hurt. Besides, in the matter of dress there could be no one better able to advise you. Although she does not care for the social round she was a famous beauty in her youth—the toast of the Town—and will know exactly what you should do."

Pippa's heart sank. Vaguely she expected Lady Cresswell to resemble the Dowager and had thought at least to armour herself in becoming and fashionable attire for the meeting with so formidable a female. But she could see that it would not do to beg off. Submissively she went upstairs to put on her hat.

Lady Cresswell lived in Kensington, and her daughter-in-law was surprised by the modesty of the establishment. No butler here, but a comfortable-looking abigail whom Quentin promptly greeted with a hug and a kiss.

"Emmy was used to be my nurse," he told Pippa, drawing her forward. "She will tell you the most apocryphal tales of my childhood and has no respect at all for my present dignities."

And as Pippa shook hands with the smiling, curtseying Emmy, "Where is Mama, Emmy? Is it safe to interrupt her?"

"Couldn't have picked a better time, milord. She's in the studio but she's only clearing up. And expecting you, of course, and her young ladyship here. Longing to see the pair of you and well pleased that you've settled to marry at last, though she *did* say that it was just like you to go about it different from anybody else."

On this encouraging note Pippa followed her husband up two pairs of stairs to the studio which occupied the entire attic floor of the house.

Anyone less like the Dowager Lady Merland would have been difficult to imagine. Like her son, Lady Cresswell was fair. The golden curls that had been so much admired in her youth were faded now, but her eyes, of a beautiful dark blue, were still lovely, and if her delicate skin showed fine lines about the mouth and eyes, its pure colouring owed nothing to artifice. She was wearing a shapeless paint-spattered smock and in one hand she clutched a dusting cloth. One certainly could not picture Lady Merland holding so homely an article, but to the nervous Pippa it was somehow reassuring.

Quentin strode in confidently, caught his mother in an enveloping hug, heedless of the danger of transferring paint smears to his elegant Town raiment, and lifted her bodily off

155

her feet, rubbing his cheek against her soft one before he turned his head to kiss her, and then perching her on the edge of a deal bench which ran the length of the room. Holding her prisoned there by one arm about her shoulders, he waved the other hand, showman fashion, towards Pippa, and announced, "There you are, Mama. I've brought you what you've always wanted."

Pippa curtsied shyly, and thought that after all there was something to be said for formal manners, since she could think of nothing to say in response to this airy introduction.

Lady Cresswell, quite as unconventional as Quentin had described her, accorded her new daughter-in-law a long, measuring look. Pippa's colour rose, but she faced it bravely enough, even though she felt as though her inmost thoughts were exposed to that penetrating glance. Her half-proffered hand sank back to her side and her head came up proudly. She had nothing to hide.

The pause seemed endless. Then Lady Cresswell said softly, "Yes. I believe you have." Her mouth curved to a smile that was wholly warm and welcoming. "But we are embarrassing the poor child. Almost I said frightening. But I do not think that she is one to be easily frightened. Give you good morning, daughter, and welcome to this haphazard and all too casual family. I hope you will find happiness with us."

She insisted that they must drink to the

future, a toast that all could share, but it did not seem to occur to her to suggest that they remove to more conventional surroundings to drink it. She remained perched on the work bench. Pippa was invited to occupy a lofty seat reminiscent of a throne, which the artist occasionally used when painting a model from life. Quentin leaned comfortably against the window frame. Emmy, coming in slightly breathless with a tray of cakes and wine, was invited to drink the toast with them, which she did with enthusiasm, though protesting that strong drink at this hour of the day might have disastrous effects on the elegant luncheon that she was preparing for them.

"Emmy is a darling," announced her mistress abruptly, as the door closed behind her. "Perhaps the finest person I know. Quite selfless and loyal to the core, but kindly and comical too. Have you ever noticed how the worthiest persons can be uncomfortable to live with if they lack a sense of humour?"

Pippa had never actually lived with such a person, but even in so small a village as Daylesford they were not unknown. "Rigid, prickly and unsympathetic," she returned promptly, "so that you come to detest their virtues and would gladly exchange them for an entertaining sinner."

"Bless the child!" exclaimed Lady Cresswell. "Precisely so! Well—Emmy is just the opposite. So comfortable and so droll that you quite forget her sheer goodness."

Pippa began to relax, feeling that she and Lady Cresswell might come to understand each other pretty well. They spent half an hour in the studio and she was skilfully encouraged to lower her guard. Lady Cresswell, showing them the series of studies which she had just completed, added a candid commentary on her work, shaking a rueful head over mediocrity here, inviting their approval of instances where she had captured exactly the impression that she had sought. Since the paintings represented London street urchins in various moods and activities, Pippa could not judge them from her knowledge of the models, but that scarcely seemed necessary. The youngsters were so vividly alive, comical or pathetic, cunning or wistful, that their veracity was beyond question. She particularly liked a sketch of two small girls solemnly dancing to the music of a street violinist, while a study of a ragged lad curled up asleep in an empty barrel with a thin mongrel pup clasped in his arms moved her almost to tears.

"Sentimental," teased Quentin. "I'm ashamed of you, Mama."

It was Pippa who rounded on him. "I believe it was exactly like that," she told him fiercely. "You can tell by the grip of his fingers in the pup's fur. Even in sleep he would not let go of his one friend and comfort."

Quentin obligingly retracted. Lady Cresswell eyed her vehement daughter-in-law with thoughtful satisfaction. It was plain that the girl had simply said what she thought with no particular intention of pleasing the artist. But the artist was inclined to be well pleased with her son's choice.

She dismissed the pair to wait for her in the dining parlour, saying that she must tidy herself before lunch or Emmy would scold, and suggesting that Quentin should entertain his wife by showing her the book of sketches that she had taken of him as a small boy. Her son declined to do any such thing, swearing that he would never be allowed to forget such an undignified exhibition, but relented on reaching the parlour, even going so far as to search out the miniature that Mama had painted of a sturdy toddler which had one of his baby curls hidden away behind it.

They lunched comfortably, the food well chosen and tempting but not oppressive by its grandeur, the hostess insisting that they should drink champagne. If married life went on like this, thought Pippa, she would soon become an inebriate. But the champagne was delicious. Perhaps it helped her to sustain the shock when Lady Cresswell said suddenly, "I must paint you."

Quentin groaned. "Oh, no, Mama. There is no time. Far more use if you were to present her. For she must be presented on her marriage, you know, and who is to do it if not you?

159

Besides, we are looking to you to give her a touch of Town bronze before she makes her come-out. There has been no opportunity for shopping, as you can well imagine. And what are we to do about her mourning?"

But Lady Cresswell, having enquired into the precise degree of relationship, was of the opinion that so long as Pippa did not *dance* during this first season, convention would be satisfied. "It is nearly six months," she counted on her fingers, "and I am sure that your uncle would not wish to make things difficult for us." And Pippa, remembering Uncle Philip's remarks on this very head, could only agree.

"As for the rest," her ladyship smiled at her son with dazzling sweetness, "I shall arrange everything. Most certainly I must paint her. And naturally I shall present her. I would not dream of yielding the privilege to any one else. In fact I shall come and stay with you at Merland House."

She considered this prospect thoughtfully for a moment, and a little smile crept about the corners of her mouth. "You will scarcely believe it, my dear," she told Pippa confidentially, "but in my day I was a considerable social success. You shall outshine me. No, don't protest. Of course you are not pretty. Thank God for it. When I have done with you, you will be beautiful, and every one will acknowledge it. I cannot imagine how my purblind son came to choose such a jewel. There must be something of the artist in him after all. So. It is settled. You may leave her with me," she nodded happily at Quentin. "We will indulge in such an orgy of shopping that you will probably have to sell out of the Funds, and no one—not even you—shall set eyes on her until my task is done. I will paint her—but I will not permit that to interfere with the amusing prospect of presenting this season's outstanding success. Give me a month—and I will astound you."

"But Mama!" protested her son. "You cannot snatch her away from me like this! We have been married only a week!"

"So much the better," retorted his unfeeling parent cheerfully. "You have not yet had time to become utterly dependent on each other. Besides it is shockingly provincial for married couples—even newly-weds—to be for ever in each other's pockets, and you may as well become accustomed. But what is more to the point, your wife will bear me out when I say that she would rather stay with me than have her servants watching every stage of her transformation from chrysalis to butterfly."

Which so chimed with Pippa's own sentiments that the matter was settled forthwith, and a somewhat disconsolate Marquess returned to his stately but surprisingly lonely mansion.

# *Eleven*

In the month that followed, Pippa learned a
great many things.

So far as the shopping expeditions were
concerned, they were not in the least what she
had expected. Instead of escorting her to those
exclusive establishments presided over by haugh-
ty modistes of the first stare, Lady Cresswell
sent Emmy out with precise instructions to
buy her one dress. It was a demure garment in
a pleasing shade of green, quite unremarkable
save for a certain quiet elegance. With it she
wore a close-fitting bonnet, and her hostess,
entering into the spirit of the thing, lent her a
veil. Thus modestly attired she accompanied
her ladyship on several visits to warehouses,
where her eyes were dazzled by the rich fabrics
that were brought out for their approval. Silks,
velvets, brocades, the finest of linen and delicate muslin, Pippa was awe-struck by the quan-

tity that her ladyship purchased without so much as a second thought.

"Furs we may leave to Quentin, and jewels, of course. Though it is in my mind that jade or topaz would better become you than old fashioned family jewellery. Now let us buy slippers and gloves and stockings. Hats can be left for the time being until we have decided the best style for your hair."

While they rested briefly between these excursions, the elder lady dispensed much worldly wisdom. "I need not warn you against being over-bold," she said once. "That is not in your nature. You are more likely to err from diffidence. You will meet a great many people, from the well-born and the wealthy to those vulgar mushrooms who hang upon the fringes of Society. Never let yourself be intimidated. It is not as if you were a raw seventeen-year-old who must wait upon the approval of the influential hostesses. You are married to a man of the first rank, and if you are not very experienced in social matters, you have good sense and good principles. Trust to those, and you will do. You *might* make a slip over precedence. It is well-nigh impossible to remember the exact standing of every member of the "ton" unless you have grown up among them. If you *should* make such a mistake, remember that anyone who shows annoyance has obviously a very inflated notion of his own consequence.

Or hers—since women are more prone to take a pet for such an imagined slight. *Never* apologise. Shrug it off with a smile if you are directly approached. For the rest, rely upon your instinct. You will naturally shrink from the vulgar and the toad-eater; you will be kind to the timid and inept. You will soon see how easy it is."

As they came to know each other more intimately, her ladyship occasionally discoursed on the married state in general and the marriage of her son in particular. By now Pippa was accustomed to her impersonal assessment and candid criticism, but when it was applied to Quentin she took fire immediately. At the mere suggestion that he had always been a little spoiled she protested vigorously.

His mother smiled tolerantly. "Easy to see that you are fathoms deep in love, my dear, and very happy I am to know it. But tell me—if you can remember so distant a time. Before you fell in love with him, did it never occur to you that he had always had whatever he desired without any effort or hardship on his part? That even his generosity—and he *is* very generous—cost him nothing, since it entailed no sacrifice?"

Pippa opened her mouth to renew her protest —and stopped. She looked absurdly guilty as she remembered that this was precisely what she *had* thought. Even before she had been aware of his lordship's identity. A carelessly kind young man who had never known what it was to go without.

Lady Cresswell smiled. "Ah! I see that you *do* remember. That is why I said that he has always been a little spoiled. There was nothing to be done about it, and it has not made him mean or greedy, but he *does* take things for granted. If you will listen to the advice of one who loves him just as dearly as you do, don't let him take *you* for granted. If you do—well—he will be kind and generous, for that is his nature, and he will always guard you well. But he will never exert himself to show you that you are the one woman in the world for him. And that, in her heart of hearts, is what a woman really needs."

From the serious expression on Pippa's face, it was easy to see that these words had struck home.

"I am not suggesting that you should set up a series of flirts, still less a regular cicisbeo. We Cresswells have always been high sticklers in that respect. Nor do I think it would be at all to *your* taste.But it will do him no harm to let it be seen that you are perfectly at home in Society and that you need never lack a creditable escort to such concerts, picnics or military reviews as it pleases you to attend."

Pippa's ingenuous countenance was a mixture of doubt and merriment. "Since my Town acquaintance is absolutely non-existent, ma'am, that will surely present some difficulty," she suggested.

"When I have done with you, the only difficulty will be to select the one who will do you most credit," said her ladyship simply.

With this laudable object in view she sent a message to her son informing him that she wished to borrow the light Town coach for a day, and told Pippa that she would have to amuse herself as best she could during her absence. "I would take you with me, but I am not sure of being able to achieve my purpose, and I would not wish to raise your hopes too high," she said mysteriously. "But I shall be back by dinner time, and perhaps I shall have a surprise for you."

Pippa spent a good deal of this idle day in meditating upon her mother-in-law's advice, and wondering how it might apply in circumstances of which that lady knew nothing. The surprise materialised in the unexpected person of Miss Pooley, a neat, bird-like little woman with bright dark eyes and a prim mouth. It was difficult to estimate what age she might be, but Pippa thought she could be in her fifties, a view that was partly confirmed when it presently emerged that at one time she had been Lady Cresswell's dresser.

"Of course I have no need of such a skilled attendant nowadays," that lady explained, while Miss Pooley was unpacking her belongings. "Emmy does all that I require. The thing is, I was not quite sure I could coax her to come to you. She is quite the top of the trees, you see, and would not demean herself by serving any commonplace female. But apart from that she is very likeable and I could see that she took a fancy to you at once. She has a distinct tendre for Quentin, too, though he used to tease her shockingly, so she would be glad to wait upon his wife. She will add enormously to your consequence. Not only will she advise you as to what you should wear on any occasion. She can accompany you when you wish to go shopping or walk in the Park, and you can rely upon her advice in any small social dilemma. Now don't look so doubtful, my love! I know you don't care for the notion of having a lady's maid always about you, but once the Season is in full swing you will find that you cannot do without. And Pooley is a perfect treasure—utterly discreet and quite unobtrusive. What is more, she is perfectly to be relied upon not to tattle to the other servants, and that is the greatest comfort, especially when one is newly married. I'd be willing to stake a handsome sum that in three months' time you will admit that you wouldn't know how to go on without her."

Pippa thought that in that case she would be a poor sort of creature, but made no audible demur. Lady Cresswell, respecting the girl's innocence, did not so much as mention the absolute necessity of employing a dresser who was, in fact, a private information service. One's personal maid, if she knew her duties, picked up all the 'on dits' from the other servants and kept her mistress informed of those that she thought essential to her welfare. Pooley had already reported to Lady Cresswell on the nature and extent of the tales that the Dowager Lady Merland had circulated about the new one. Quentin had married an ignorant country miss, out of some notion of chivalry. That was the kindest version. Another said that he had been trapped into marriage by a cunning wench who had portrayed innocence all too cleverly, while a third, more malicious still, hinted that there was an all too solid reason for this ill-assorted marriage, and that it would be very interesting to mark the birth date of the new heir. She had understood from Mr. Anstey, her late employer's butler, explained Pooley, her prim air more disinterested than ever, that the gentlemen were already laying bets in the clubs as to the imminence of this event.

Lady Cresswell had smiled contentedly. Whatever else she might be, her new daughter-in-law was not pregnant. Joyously she planned her own campaign.

"Sheer jealousy. Just because Quentin did not fall into her carefully baited trap. And who could blame him? I say nothing against Flora

Smalley. A pretty child, and well-mannered. But a mere rush-light compared with my lovely Philippa. It is no wonder that Quentin was swept clear off his feet. Oh, yes! Of excellent blood, of course. An ancient Scottish family on the mother's side—a Merchiston—connected with the Napiers, and through them, I believe, with Montrose."

That was what she would say. She was distinctly vague about that last statement, but even in this prosaic age the great Marquess's name still sounded trumpets, and she was sure he would have been perfectly willing to come to the aid of a fellow country-woman. On the father's side there was no need for airy subterfuge. The Langley pedigree was as long as English history and would silence any doubters. Lady Cresswell found it vastly amusing that her worldly wise son was still quite unaware that his wife had inherited a substantial portion of Langley wealth.

Two weeks of hectic activity ensued. Sewing maids arrived and were installed in the studio, where, under Pooley's direction, they set to work on the creation of dresses such as Pippa had never dreamed of. Pooley sketched and cut and fitted, the girls stitched, and Lady Cresswell commended and criticised and suggested the occasional alteration, while Pippa stood meekly under the ministering hands, revolved obediently when bidden, and stared in wonder at the unrecognisable reflection in the long glass.

She had studied a great many fashion journals since her arrival in Town, but she could trace little resemblance between the gowns that were taking shape in the studio and the illustrations in their pages. Once she ventured to voice her doubts. Pooley smiled, her tight prim little smile. Lady Cresswell explained kindly, "My dear, you will *set* the fashions, not follow them. Those"—she nodded at the carriage dress that Pooley was fitting and at an evening gown that Belinda held over her arm awaiting Pooley's approval—"will undoubtedly figure in next year's styles."

When she was not actually required by the busy workers, Pippa was occupied in directing piles of invitations to a Dress Ball to be held at Merland House. Lady Cresswell had arranged for her to be presented at the first of the season's Drawing Rooms. Once that ordeal was over she would be fairly launched on her social career. The prospect terrified her. She felt like a puppet, compelled to dance against her will because an irresistible power pulled the strings, but when she spoke of nervous qualms, Lady Cresswell was brisk and matter-of-fact. "You will have nothing to do but smile pleasantly— and hide your amazement at some of Society's oddities," she said. "Mrs. Dunstable is an excellent housekeeper. You may safely leave the catering arrangements in her hands, and I will help you over the decorations. Quentin will be with you to receive the guests and there can be

171

no doubt that the whole thing will be a great success. Just wait until your gowns are finished and you will see that you need do no more than accept the tributes evoked by your appearance with due graciousness."

Pippa felt that there must be more to social success than *that*, but she was only too happy to defer judgement.

And when the first half dozen gowns were completed she was actually almost a little frightened at the change in her appearance. That colours and fabrics should have been chosen to set off her colouring and draw attention to a delightful figure was no more than one would expect of an artist of Lady Cresswell's calibre. It was the new personality that the dresses created for her that startled Pippa. Created—or released? For she had to admit that she felt perfectly at home in this new splendour. She had always been accustomed to thinking of herself as passably pleasant-looking, neatly and suitably dressed. Who could have dreamed that beneath that unlikely façade there lay hidden a princess out of a legend? For the usually modest Pippa was obliged to admit that that was the first thought that sprang to mind when she surveyed the image in the glass. Certainly it was not workaday Pippa Langley. But it could well be Philippa Cresswell, the new Marchioness of Merland—who might, perhaps, be expected to look like royalty.

It must be confessed that she gazed and gazed; and turned again eagerly to the glass as each new dress was tried, half fearful lest the strange magic should have lost its power. But the enchantment held; and the contented smile on Lady Cresswell's face, the smug satisfaction on Pooley's, were confirmation sufficient of her own tremulous delight.

The whole effect had been very skilfully contrived. There was nothing exaggerated or in questionable taste. The departure from the current mode was partly a matter of cut and line, partly a complete absence of meretricious trimmings. Very high waists were all the crack, but Pippa's mentors were united in insisting that it would be positively sinful not to draw attention to a tiny waist and delectable curves, so the dresses had been cut with a waistline no more than an inch higher than nature had intended. That inch, together with a slight lengthening of the skirts, which, in the evening gowns, extended to a tiny train, made her look taller, gave her that hint of regality. This idea had been followed in all the dresses. Otherwise, of course, they were all different. The court gown, fashioned out of a golden brocade patterned with tiny glinting sea-horses, had a low décolletage and sleeves so small that they were a mere twist of fabric across the beautifully moulded arms.

"Just to show we've nothing to hide," announced her ladyship, with the blunt honesty to which Pippa was becoming accustomed. "Skin, shoulders, throat—all flawless," and in an access of fervour that was less familiar, "My child, you are God's gift to an artist—and to a deserving dresser," she threw in obligingly, with a gamin grin at Pooley. "As raw material for our skills, you are ideal."

Which didn't do a great deal for one's self confidence, reflected Pippa. Unfortunately she *felt* like raw material. *Very* raw. And wondered for the hundredth time how her husband was faring, and if he missed her and regretted their untimely separation.

Of all the beautiful materials that they had purchased, Lady Cresswell had selected Pippa's favourite for her first ball gown. A thick, supple taffeta, the colour of a chestnut but lightly veined with gold, it turned her hair, assiduously polished by Pooley's faithful brushing, into a living, glowing glory that almost matched its own fiery hue, and was cut more like a coat than a dress. When Pippa, though sunk in adoration, ventured to suggest that it did not look much like a ball gown, Lady Cresswell explained that it was an adaptation of a Chinese mandarin's robe. It had a high upstanding collar—which emphasized the lovely line of the wearer's throat—and long loose sleeves, ending at the curve of the elbow in front, but descending in deep points almost to hem level on the underside. It opened down the front to

174

reveal an underdress in deep apricot-tinted tulle—a fabric completely new to Pippa—softer than silk and finer than the finest muslin. The sleeves of the gown were lined with it, too, and tantalising glimpses of the lighter colour were revealed when the wearer raised her arms.

"Almost a pity that you will not be dancing," was Lady Cresswell's comment. "Though as you say, it is not really designed for that. A hostess gown, rather, and one that will not soon be forgotten." And Pippa twinkled at her naughtily and asked whether it was the gown or the hostess that merited this accolade.

Two days later Lady Cresswell decreed that the time had come to remove to Merland House. "You have dresses enough for several days and others nearing completion. The maids will be kept busy for two or three weeks yet, but it is time that you and I bestirred ourselves. *You* must accustom yourself to the formality that is inescapable in Town, and *I* must seek out some of my old friends and have them put the word about that my new daughter-in-law is something quite out of the common run."

She laughed at Pippa's horrified protests, but relented sufficiently to explain that, while it would not be proper for the girl to attend large parties until after her presentation, it would be quite in order for her to accompany her mother-in-law when that lady paid morning calls.

"They will not be very exciting," she warned.

That gamin grin betrayed her. "I have other friends, of a more Bohemian kind. Much more amusing. The ones to whom I plan to introduce you are the pillars of Society. Not its leaders, you notice. They would never do anything so dashing. But they are the ones whose approbation you must win. And there is no need for *that* frightened face. You have only to be yourself—a pleasant, well-mannered young woman of attractive appearance, dressed in the most exquisite taste. Intelligent, but not so cock-a-hoop as to think that you know better than your elders, and actually willing to learn of them. Very well pleased to be in London and enjoying *their* society. All of which you can do without effort or falsehood."

Pippa thought it over. "Well—if I may say so without undue conceit," she conceded, with that engaging twinkle, "all but the last. They *do* sound rather intimidating."

Lady Cresswell shook her head. "No. Stiff, but kind. You cannot suppose that I would claim them as friends if they were not. It is just that they have their standards of moral rectitude and proper behaviour, and will not tolerate any laxity."

She appeared to ponder this pronouncement for a moment, and suddenly giggled. "Do you know? It has just occurred to me that if I had not more or less withdrawn from the social round in favour of my painting, I should prob-

176

ably be one of them. Quite as stiff-necked, and, I trust, as kind."

Pippa laughed with her at this comical notion, and her anxieties were a little allayed. It was agreed that they should remove to Merland House on the following day.

His lordship, meanwhile, had not been idle. Slightly disgruntled by his Mama's calm appropriation of his wife, he had sought diversion in selecting horses and a carriage that would serve the needs of a fashionable young matron. She was a competent horsewoman, so it was a comparatively simple matter to select a couple of nice-looking well-mannered hacks. When it came to choosing a carriage it was a little more complicated. There was already a landau, practically new, which they could use for all Town purposes when they wished to be driven. But if he knew his Pippa she would wish to drive herself whenever it was possible, and although she was accustomed to handling a gig, sporting carriages, even when designed for a lady to drive, were a very different matter. He viewed a crane-necked phaeton longingly. It was so much more elegant than the ordinary perch variety and he did not want his wife to be thought dowdy, but her safety must come first. The astute salesman suggested that the safer vehicle could always be exchanged for something more dashing if her ladyship disliked it, and the bargain was struck.

Next came the search for a pair of match geldings that should be sufficiently lively without being too strong for a lady. This was a long business, for he was very particular in his requirements. It was a pity that he had just driven down into Kent to inspect a pair that sounded promising when his mother and wife descended on Merland House. Since they were accompanied by Emmy, Pooley and three sewing maids, and a third carriage was needed to convey the numerous trunks and band-boxes, it was quite an imposing cavalcade, but Mrs. Dunstable accepted the invasion with perfect sang-froid, behaviour which constrasted strongly with the startled expression which she bestowed upon her young mistress when Pippa, who had lingered to bestow a quite unnecessary vail upon a crossing sweeper because he looked hungry, followed her mama-in-law into the house. She herself described the incident with considerable dramatic talent to the assembled company in the housekeeper's room that night.

"Proper taken aback, I was. Never seen such a change in any one. Indeed I'd not have known her if she hadn't smiled and greeted me by name. A pretty voice she has, and a rare bonny smile, but my! What a difference the right clothes can make. She'll take the Town by storm, the way she looks now. See if I'm not right."

Since the select gathering of the senior members of the household included both Emmy and Pooley, this pronouncement took very well.

As for his lordship's absence, his mother declared that they would do very well without him. Indeed, since the business of the next few days was wholly feminine, he would really have been very much in the way.

No one thought to enquire into Pippa's feelings on the subject.

# Twelve

She had scant opportunity to brood over this latest coincidence in the chain of minor obstacles that appeared to have been specially designed to keep husband and wife apart. Having attained the sanctuary of her own room, she *did* study her reflection in the glass with a wry grimace for the beautiful gown so carefully selected with a view to impressing a casual spouse. But she had barely time to take off her bonnet before Pooley was there to preside over the delicate business of unpacking and bestowing her clothes, watching jealously to ensure that any hint of crease or wrinkle was carefully pressed out before the gowns were hung away. So there was nothing to do but wander downstairs rather disconsolately and seek distraction in a book until it was time to submit herself to the maid's ministrations; the skilful application of sweet-scented lotions to her skin; the brushing, pomading and careful arrangement of her hair—all the long-drawn out ritual of changing her gown for dinner.

There was much that was pleasant and interesting in her new way of life, she decided, idly turning the pages in a book of engravings, but there could be no denying that the business of being an ornament to Society was a shocking waste of time. If there had not been a certain neglectful gentleman to be surprised—stunned, even—by his wife's dazzling appearance, she would have been sorely tempted to abandon the whole scheme. There were so many more interesting and delightful activities to be enjoyed, especially now that she was in London. She remembered her girlish dreams of all that she would do if ever such an opportunity came her way, and the plans that she and Quentin had made together. From the programme that Lady Cresswell had outlined for her, it did not seem that there would be much time for the expeditions they had discussed.

There was none. If she was not driving with her mama-in-law in the park or paying morning calls on influential females who must be satisfied as to her claims to gentility, she was being fitted for yet more dresses or changing her gown in order to attend a theatre or to make one of a 'quiet conversible party' at the house of one of the said influential females. She sincerely appreciated all that her sponsor was trying to do for her and did her best to bring credit upon her teachers, but it was really dreadfully dull. Even the evenings spent at the theatre could scarcely be counted as entertainment. First and foremost they were social occasions, with a great deal of coming and going between the boxes, continual introductions, names only half heard, a good deal of inconsequential chatter and very little opportunity to enjoy the drama without interruption.

And alas! Her truant lord, when he did at last return, was not in the least stunned or dazzled by her transformation. He *did* go so far as to compliment her on being in high bloom, suggesting that the air of Town must agree with her constitution. He also apologised for being away when she came home, and enquired when it would be convenient for her to inspect the horses that had been the cause of his seeming neglect. He trusted that when she had done so, she would find herself quite in charity with him once more.

In fact he was so very formal and polite that she began to wonder if she had somehow displeased him. He had never before seemed so remote and unapproachable. She was quite thankful when Lady Cresswell came in to interrupt the brief tête-à-tête.

How could she guess that his lordship, arriving betimes and informed that the ladies had strolled out into the gardens to see the spring flowers, had gone at once in search of them? Or know that he had wondered momentarily as to the identity of the elegant creature who was walking with Mama and then looked about him in search of his wife. And then Pippa had laughed—that infectious gurgle of merriment that always made him smile in sympathy, even when he had not heard the joke—and he had realised the truth. Engrossed in their conversation—Lady Cresswell was indulging a regrettable talent for neat and caustic characterisation—the two had not noticed his approach, and he was able to withdraw unseen, with a strong feeling that he would prefer to assimilate the new state of affairs in private.

Mama had been as good as her word. So much was obvious. She had said that she would astound him; that she would groom his wife to become the success of the Season—and she had done just that. But in the process Pippa had become a stranger. So changed that he had not recognised her. And the sensation was not a pleasant one. The more he considered it, the less he liked it. It might be a very fine thing to have a wife who was a great social success; to be the envy of all one's friends. But he begged leave to doubt it. In the month that had elapsed since he left her with his mother, he had missed his wife more than he had thought possible. But it was his loveable, familiar Pippa that he had missed, not some well-groomed, well-drilled Society diamond, with all the natural warmth and personality hidden by the public façade. And yet—he hesitated. Women set much store on such things. If Pippa's heart was set on a brilliant Season, it would be selfish to deny her, though his impulse was to snatch her away, back to rural seclusion, where he could have her to himself. He supposed, in any case, that he could scarcely interfere at this stage, with her presentation arranged and invitations sent out for a ball. Better to let things ride. His assumption of an unfamiliar formality was as much a mask for doubt and uncertainty as was Pippa's newly acquired sophistication.

Unfortunately it was all too easy to maintain a purely surface relationship in that vast and servant-ridden mansion. It was still staffed in accordance with the dowager's notions of consequence, since Quentin had been too easy-going to reduce the establishment to more normal proportions. Lady Cresswell complained that if you so much as dropped your table napkin, two footmen bumped their heads together to pick it up while a third hastened to supply you with a clean one, and though this was, of course, an exaggeration, it was quite true that an atmosphere of intimacy was not easy to achieve. The industry and devotion to duty displayed by every member of the staff, not one of whom wished to lose a comfortable and well-paid position, made private conversation practically impossible, since fires were tended, candles trimmed and curtains adjusted about every ten minutes. Or so it seemed to his lordship, anxious at least to establish himself on easier terms with his wife. He *did* succeed in persuading her to drive out with him in the new phaeton, but although her pleasure in this acquisition was very gratifying, the expedition itself did nothing to forward his purpose, since at least half of his acquaintance seemed to have chosen the same time to drive in the Park and he was frequently obliged to break off his attempts to engage his wife in conversation in order to return their greetings and perform the necessary introductions. It struck him that his friends were excessively delighted to renew his acquaintance and he had no hesitation in ascribing this sudden enthusiasm to the delightful appearance presented by his companion. It gave him no satisfaction at all. If those fellows imagined that they had to deal with a complaisant husband who would not object to his wife's conducting elegant flirtations with such dashing young blades as took her fancy, they should soon discover their mistake.

One further attempt he made to cross the intangible barrier that seemed to have arisen between them. On an evening when, for once, they had dined quietly at home, he braced himself to stroll nonchalantly into Pippa's room some ten minutes or so after she had bidden him a dutiful good night. It was unfortunate that Pooley should have chosen the same evening to try which of several hair styles would best support Court feathers. A lady with half her head in such formidable array would scarcely be in the mood to welcome intimate approaches. The marquess hastily formulated an innocuous enquiry about the time of tomorrow's drive, and retreated to await a more propitious opportunity.

Pippa dressed for the Drawing Room in a daze of fright. Her cheeks were burning, her hands icy. Not even the lovely golden gown could revive her quaking confidence. What had she, commonplace Philippa Langley, to say to a Queen? Not that she *was* Philippa Langley any longer. For a moment she almost wished she was. Then there would be no terrifying ordeal to face. But beyond today's ceremonies lay the possibility of the future on which her heart was set. *If* she achieved the success that Lady Cresswell so confidently predicted, it might serve to draw her husband into the ranks of her admirers.

At least that forlorn little hope gave her the determination to go through with it. She watched Pooley dress her hair high over the pads that would make a secure foundation for her feathers. Normally she hated pads. They made her head feel hot and her neck stiff. But the thought of feathers tilting ridiculously from side to side as she performed her successive curtsies to such lesser royalties as might be present was quite sufficient to ensure her submission today. Two feathers only, decreed Lady Cresswell. Some ladies, volunteered Pippa, wore as many as five or six—or so she had been told.

"And look like circus ponies from Astley's," returned her mama-in-law acidly.

Pippa's feathers were of modest dimensions, but they had been dyed to an exact match for her gown and they curled becomingly from the topaz circlet that Lady Cresswll had preferred to more costly jewels. It was more important to their wearer that they should stay secure. Pooley, calming her feverish anxiety, assured her that everyone felt just the same; that she would neither drop her bouquet nor trip over her skirt, while nothing short of a dead faint would dislodge the feathers.

"And then you wouldn't know anything about it," contributed Lady Cresswell cheerfully, and insisted that she drink a glass of sherry, assuring her that no, of course the Queen wouldn't smell it on her breath. She wouldn't be near enough—and in any case Her Majesty was addicted to snuff and it was doubtful if she would notice anything less pungent than that. Pippa, much shocked at what seemed to her no better than lésé-majesté, drank obediently, and felt the better for it.

And in the event her presentation passed off quite smoothly. None of the nightmarish events that she had dreaded occurred to mar it. The Queen bestowed a gracious smile upon her, and two of the princesses engaged her in conversation on the topic of her mama-in-law's painting. It was a little disappointing that the Prince of Wales should not be present but, as Lady Cresswell pointed out, this was only to be expected, since he was known to be on bad terms with his parents. Best of all, in Pippa's private opinion, was her husband's gravely expressed view that she looked very lovely. "A credit to you, Mama, and to all of us."

Nevertheless she was thankful to be safely back in her own room with Pooley removing her feathers and suggesting that she might like to wear her court gown for the dinner party that was to round off the day's festivities. "With a scarf of gold net laid about your shoulders it will be perfectly appropriate," pronounced the dresser, "seeing as it's quite a large party with a lot of important guests."

Pippa let her have her way. "It's funny, isn't it?" she confided thoughtfully. "The dinner party doesn't frighten me now. I suppose that's the whole point of being presented. If you can go through *that,* you can face any other social occasion with fortitude." And Pooley, who in her time had presided over the débuts of half a dozen terrified neophytes, agreed indulgently that there might be a good deal in what she said.

Perhaps Pippa's theory was sound. Certainly in the weeks that followed she achieved all

and more than her sponsor had hoped. She had
no claim to classical beauty, but since she was
always dressed to make the most of her good
points, with a faint hint of the unusual or the
exotic carefully planned to rivet the beholder's
attention, she was generally held to be very
handsome. Her social behaviour, which owed
nothing to artifice or careful drilling, could
scarely have been bettered. She had outgrown
the gaucherie of the average débutante and
bore herself with a serene dignity that delighted
her mother-in-law, since it held no trace of self
consequence. Because of her simply country
background the pleasures of the Season were
all fresh and new. She was never bored. And
since she was intelligent and well-read she
could converse sensibly on most topics. What
was even more important, she could listen with
understanding and sympathy even when her
own knowledge was limited. A more than pre-
sentable female who is also a good listener can
usually command social success. When she is
presented to Society by a consummate artist
and the details of her impeccable lineage, her
handsome fortune and the romantic circumstances of her marriage have been skilfully
put about in the right circles, that success be-
comes assured. Even the enmity of the Dowager Lady Merland served to enhance Pippa's
popularity. That lady was little liked. Her spiteful tales were very rightly ascribed to jealousy,

and a number of people to whom she had given offence were quietly pleased that she had failed to trap her nephew for little Miss Flora. No one had anything against the girl herself, a pretty child and likeable. It was a sad pity that her chaperone should have alienated so many people.

Before the month was out it was becoming increasingly difficult for Pippa to choose between the invitations that were showered on her, for no one could comfortably manage more than three parties in one day. At the Merland House ball—one of the Season's most triumphant successes—the shocking fact emerged that some family bereavement debarred her young ladyship from dancing. Overnight it became the fashion for her would-be partners to request instead the favour of a stroll in the conservatory or a leisurely inspection of such ivories, miniatures, china figurines or other objets d'art as their host and hostess favoured. These activities were perfectly proper, since there were always a number of older people who did not care to dance similarly engaged, but it could not be denied that they offered far more opportunity for intimate conversation than was possible on the dance floor, where the changing figures were for ever separating partners and every one in the set could hear what was said. It was regrettable though, in the opinion of several romantically inclined gentlemen, that the lady seemed disinclined to make the most of these favourable circumstances. She was perfectly pleasant and approachable, but she seemed to have no taste for amatory dalliance. If you talked of your family, your country pursuits or your military ambitions, she was the most delightful companion that a man could wish, appearing to enter into your feelings with perfect understanding. But if you launched out into complimentary hyperbole, comparing her to some classic goddess or pagan queen, your efforts were more likely to be greeted with a giggle or a sharp setdown.

The only person who seemed to be unaware of this sad deficiency in the lady's otherwise admirable social qualities was her husband. That gentleman was thought to view his wife's court with a quite ridiculously jealous eye. He could generally be found prowling in her vicinity, unless a particularly determined hostess had succeeded in directing his attentions to one of her less popular female guests. Indeed one young gentleman, more imaginative than his fellows, declared that the glare in Merland's eyes reminded him of the light that flickered from a sword blade, and was more circumspect in his approach thereafter. He even accepted in good part the jeers of his fellows.

"Cow-hearted? Well, to make no bones about it, the fellow's a damn fine swordsman. I've no wish to meet him with *that* look in his eye—and only for following the fashion. For that's all it is y'know. And when all's said and done, she *is* his wife. But as to cow-hearted—well let's see now. I'll take on any one who cares to repeat that opinion. Bare knuckles or gloves, it makes no matter, but unlike Merland I'm not in a killing humour."

He was not far out in his assessment of the situation. Since his wife, despite all the attention paid to her, showed no sign, even to a jealous eye, of developing a tendre for any other gentleman. Quentin was not precisely in killing humour, but certainly his patience had been stretched to its limit. He had given up all thought of seeking a rapprochement for the present. At the back of his mind was a vague hope that they would not, in future, need to spend the whole of every Season in Town. He had never before found the crammed programme of social functions in the least restrictive. But a life that did not permit a lady any time to devote to her lawful spouse was not the life for him. It was not that he would wish to deny Pippa any rational enjoyment. She had always seemed perfectly happy in the country, he reflected hopefully. Perhaps a month or even two in Town, just so that they should not rusticate entirely. And then, of course, if they were to set up a nursery—well—no one could deny that the country was the place for children.

He would carry his wife back to Merland at the earliest date that decency permitted, and he only hoped that Mama would not fulfil her promise—threat—of accompanying them. She had never chosen to visit the place in all the months since he had inherited. What should move her to do so now, when, to put it bluntly, her presence would be yet another hindrance in his path?

Fortunately Mama decided to stay in Town for the present. She had made a number of studies for her portrait of Pippa, but the exigencies of the social round had obliged her to abandon the task for the time being. She would go home, she announced, and work on it for a week or so, and join them later at Merland to add the final touches. Quentin heaved a sigh of relief and began to reckon how many days remained to be endured.

Word reached them that Cousin Claudia had been safely delivered of a son. Her parents were to come to Merland to carry her home as soon as she was strong enough to travel. Doubtless they would stay for several days. There were letters, too, from Cindy and Denise, full of eager plans for the summer holidays. Perhaps the last holiday that they would all share before Dickon went off to join the army, said Pippa pensively. It seemed to Quentin that a veritable horde of people was planning a descent on Merland, and each and every one of them intent on taking up his wife's time and attention.

Enough was enough. He listened to the suggestions in the various letters, smiled agreeably when his wife made tentative plans—and proceeded quietly to make his own arrangements.

# Thirteen

When Pippa had first arrived in the Metropolis, Lady Cresswell had been anxious lest some careless prattle-box should let fall in her hearing a hint as to the spiteful tales that the Dowager was putting about, but with the passing of the weeks this concern had faded. The tales themselves were so obviously exaggerated that they had been more or less laughed out of court. Which was fortunate, since with the widening of Pippa's circle of friends and the number of engagements that had crowded in upon them it became impossible for her to be forever at the girl's elbow to ward off possible danger. In any case, she told herself comfortably, Pippa was far too sensible to let herself be distressed by such silly fabrications. Any last lingering doubt was banished when her protegée went from success to success. A girl who was the toast of the town, who held court like a princess at every function that she attended, and whose husband, while keeping modestly in the background, was always at hand to lend his support, would never permit a pack of malicious lies to shake her confidence or cloud her happiness.

She could have been right. Pippa *had* a good deal of common sense. But during recent months her equable disposition had been put to severe tests. A marriage that was no true marriage was difficult enough. In addition to this she had also been subjected to the fatigue and nervous strain of a first Season. The need to study and assess her husband's reactions to her progress without appearing to do so was another turn of the screw. Instead of sleeping tranquilly the night through as had been her wont, she lay awake for hours, turning over in her mind his every word and expression, trying to decide whether or no she was making any headway. From sheer weariness she came to distrust her own judgement, and when Quentin's grave courtesy showed no sign of yielding to a warmer attitude she took fright and began to feel that she had made a mistake in accepting his offer of marriage. She had done all that she could to turn herself into the kind of wife who would do him credit—and in return he seemed to grow colder and more reserved with every passing day. Instead of growing closer, as she had so fondly hoped, they met almost as strangers. It became more and more of a strain to preserve the pose of gentle serenity, of complete contentment with her lot. There were moments when she longed to cast herself into her husband's arms and sob out her loneliness and her fears for the future. But he would probably be embarrassed by such an exhibition of feminine vapours. He would be kind—considerate. He always was. But the strong arms would hold her with impersonal gentleness when what she needed was to be ruthlessly hugged and kissed until she was breathless.

So the discovery that her husband had offered for her because he felt himself obliged to do so could scarcely have been worse timed. It came about in the simplest way and in a fashion that stamped it as very truth, in no way ascribable to deliberate malice. As débutantes it was inevitable that she and Flora Smalley should frequently find themselves attending the same parties, though they were not particularly intimate. Having had a taste of the Dowager's quality, Pippa felt rather sorry for the younger girl, while Flora, for her part, had conceived a girlish admiration for one whom she had seen emerge triumphant from a campaign of vilification.

On the fatal occasion they had both been members of a lively party of young people who had set out to spend a day in Epping Forest. They had enjoyed themselves very much, visiting a gipsy encampment where the ladies had exclaimed and giggled over having their fortunes told and then, after an alfresco lunch, hiring donkeys from the gipsies to explore the narrow forest paths. There was a good deal of light-hearted fun, the gentlemen laying bets on the qualities of their selected mounts—the fastest over a given distance—the most obstinate—the smoothest ride—the one with the nippiest pair of heels (which last caused a good deal of speculation as to precisely what the rider meant) but eventually the undignified cavalcade moved off on an exploration that any strict chaperone must have deplored. Because of the varying paces of the shaggy mounts it naturally split up into a number of small groups. And as the forest paths diverged, so the groups scattered. It was natural enough that Quentin should remain in attendance on his wife, but Flora joined them under a certain amount of duress, her particular cavalier having selected a beast of decided temperament. After several differences of opinion between donkey and rider, the animal had finally emerged victor, bearing him off along an overgrown path where his protests and objurgations could be heard receding into the distance.

The novelty of donkey riding soon palled. The little animals were very attractive to look at, with their long, curling lashes and demure expressions, but their behaviour was unpredictable and as they warmed up their pungent smell became quite overpowering. When Quentin, who had preferred to trust to his own long legs, suggested that they should turn back, the ladies were quite agreeable.

Unfortunately they had not gone very far before there was a flash of lightning, followed almost immediately by a sharp crack of thunder. In the depth of the forest no one had realised how swiftly the weather had changed. Perhaps the imminence of the storm accounted for the intractable behaviour of the donkeys, for its breaking seemed to drive them frantic. Luckily they were so small that the girls managed to slip to the ground without mishap, since Quentin had his hands full in controlling the frightened creatures.

"Better make for the gipsy camp,"he called to them between his struggles. " 'Fraid we're in for a wetting, but we must get away from the trees."

The girls followed him as best they could. The donkeys were more amenable now that their heads were turned towards home but had to be soothed after each rumble of thunder. The storm seemed to be moving away, but now the rain began to fall in earnest and it was not long before it penetrated the sheltering foliage and began to descend on them in steady streams. They were thankful indeed to reach the dubious shelter of the gipsy camp, but as it had been arranged that the carriages should pick them up at a rendezvous some distance away, their troubles were not yet over.

After some discussion with one of the grand-mothers of the tribe, during which the lady's hand was crossed with golden guineas in place of the traditional silver, Quentin left his charges in the old woman's care and went off to find the carriages.

Their hostess seemed well disposed, though they had difficulty in following her speech. She brought out a shawl and a piece of blanket that seemed reasonably clean, and indicated that they might like to take off their wet pelisses and put the dry wraps round their shoulders. This done, she offered them a share of a savoury stew, but since neither was hungry she uttered a disapproving grunt and went off to finish her own meal in more congenial company.

Left alone, the pair settled down to wait with what patience they might for Quentin's return. They were not exactly afraid, but to be left in such a situation without masculine pro-tection was not what they were accustomed to. Even the older and more independent Pippa was very thankful for Miss Smalley's companion-ship, while the timid and sheltered Flora vowed that she would have been quite senseless with terror if dear Lady Merland had not been with her.

Presently, being left undisturbed, their nerv-ous qualms abated. They grew bold enough to smile at the odd appearance that they presented and to wonder how the rest of the party was faring. The ice once broken they chatted in desultory fashion, comparing notes on the various functions that they had attended. Flora, who was beginning to adopt some of the languid airs that her friends considered the hallmark of sophistication, confided that she was to go to Brighton for a month.

"I shall be quite thankful to say farewell to Town," she announced, with a world-weary air that made Pippa smile a little. "It is become quite tedious. So hot and dusty, and none but 'Cits' left. The way they ogle one in the Park is really quite shocking."

"From all that I hear you will find Brighton just as bad. Not dusty, perhaps. But Quentin tells me that even gentlemen of the highest rank do not disdain to spy upon the ladies when they venture to bathe. And what is worse, they actually use telescopes to do it!"

Flora pretended to be suitably horrified but went on to say that she expected to enjoy herself very much. "When do you return to Merland?" she enquired politely.

"In three days' time. And like you I shall be glad to leave Town."

Flora looked a little doubtful. "Well—of course you are married, and I daresay that makes a great deal of difference. For my part, I have always found the country dreadfully dull."

As well she might, thought Pippa, with such a dragon in charge of her. No doubt the local gentry and their simple parties would be quite beneath the Dowager's touch, and the poor child had been obliged to spend a dreary existence in attendance on her starched-up aunt.

"You must come over to Merland," she said kindly. "My cousin Dickon is about your age, though Denise and Cindy are younger. There were some splendid parties last year, and picnics and riding excursions. Quentin invites all his young cousins and their friends. Last year Cousin Claudia played hostess for him but this time it will fall to me. I am sure you would enjoy being with younger people, rather than cooped up with your Aunt all the time. Perhaps she would allow you to stay with us for a week or two. That would save you the bother of driving backward and forward each day and would let you join in the games and charades and dancing at night without having to worry about keeping her out of her bed till all hours."

Flora's transparent young face lit to delight. "It would be wonderful," she breathed. "I would like it of all things. How kind of"—She broke off, the bright face clouding so swiftly that she looked near to weeping.

"She would never let me," she said tragically.

Pippa looked so taken aback that some explanation was obviously called for. Flora flushed uncomfortably and said hesitantly, "She is—is very rigid. Once she has pronounced an opinion on someone, she will never recant."

Pippa still stared at her curiously. Flora fidgetted with the fringe of the gipsy's shawl and went on, "Of course nobody believes the stories she told about you. Behind her back people laugh at her. But Aunt Sophronia will never yield an inch. She isn't really my aunt actually. She's a second cousin of Mama's. But I always call her Aunt and she has been very good to me. There are four of us at home, you see, and Mama could never have brought me out in such style."

Her words were tumbling out in a swift inconsequent flood because there was something rather frightening about Lady Merland's expression. Flora felt that she must go on chattering to bridge an awkward gap, but invention failed her and she faltered into silence.

Pippa said quietly, "I collect that her ladyship does not consider me a fit person to associate with you. Perhaps you will be so good as to tell me more about these tales that no one believes."

Flora looked more miserable than ever, but as Pippa said no more but simply waited for her reply she eventually mumbled, "Well mostly they're about your being a scheming nobody who set a clever trap for his lordship so that he was obliged to offer for you. But truly nobody believes it. I mean everybody knows that you're not a nobody. And as for his lordship being obliged to offer for you, well they can see that, too. That it's not true, I mean. Every one says that he is truly devoted and that it is an ideal marriage."

Most of this earnest apologia passed over

205

Pippa's head. She had whitened a little at the opening statement but had accepted the shock and the hurt with hard-held control. At the moment there was nothing else to be done. Somehow she must conceal from this innocent the serious nature of the blow.

"Well if that is what she believes," she managed, with an artificial little laugh, "I am sure one cannot wonder at it that she considers me unfit to take charge of younger girls. It is a pity that her misapprehension should deprive you of some pleasant parties, but I quite understand that being so much in her debt you would not wish to cause her any distress by setting up your will in opposition to hers. Did you say that you had sisters? Do, pray, tell me about them."

# *Fourteen*

The soaking that she had got in the forest made an adequate reason for excusing herself from a theatre party and retiring early. Lady Cresswell commended her prudence, "For it would never do to be taking a chill just now, with so much to be done," instructed Pooley to see that she had a hot drink as soon as she was snug between sheets, and suggested that she swallow a few drops of laudanum to ensure a good night's sleep. "For I do not scruple to tell you, my dear, that you are looking distinctly hagged."

Pippa declined the laudanum, saying that Uncle Philip had always deplored its use save in dire extremity, but admitted that she *was* feeling very tired. She would perhaps take breakfast in bed and excuse herself from riding out with her husband next morning. Lady Cresswell obligingly offering to give him a message to this effect, she was able to count on a period of undisturbed solitude in which to come to terms with her situation.

Oddly enough, now that the blow had fallen she was much calmer. She was even able to see, in the light of her new sophistication, that her own conduct had been at fault. There had certainly been grounds for some of those tales that Flora had described. Those frequent meetings that had followed on Quentin's return from France had been unwise to say the least of it, however innocent.

But there was little point, at this stage, in allotting praise or blame. It was what was to be done *now* that was important. Because of her naive folly—and even now she could not bring herself to acknowledge that Quentin was at least equally at fault—her husband had found himself in a position where he had felt obliged to offer for her. She spared a moment's thought for the stories that must have gone about in Daylesford, and wondered how they had come to Quentin's ears. Probably from the Dowager—though that lady could not have guessed how he would react! Neighbours might look askance —might smile, indulgently or slyly according to disposition, but few would be so strongly moved as to approach either of the principals in the affair directly. Yes, undoubtedly the Dowager—and how furious she must have been at the result of her meddling!

She remembered her own faint uneasiness at the—yes—almost furtive nature of the wedding arrangements, and understood at last her impression that every one had been vastly relieved when it was accomplished. Of course. Her friends had all known the urgent need for the ceremony that made an honest woman of her. It was an infuriating thought, but there was nothing to be done about it now. What she had to do was to find a way out of the tangle. Quentin must be freed, she was in no doubt on *that* head, but how best to go about it? Disappearing was no good, for that would still leave him tied to her. In any case, his notions of proper conduct would probably send him hotfoot in search of her. There was a divorce, but that was a long slow business. She had a vague idea that it entailed getting an Act passed through Parliament. And every fibre of her being shrank from the thought of the shameful publicity. There would be no hope of arranging such a matter quietly, for Quentin was a prominent figure in the world of fashion, and she herself had made something of a hit. Their perfectly commonplace comings and goings were frequently the subject of newspaper comment.

For a few desperate moments she even contemplated the possibility of counterfeiting her own death—either by accident or suicide—but it was soon seen that this was too complicated. She did not feel herself competent to deceive the whole of her acquaintance—and what would happen to Dickon and Lucinda?

She came eventually to the conclusion that

the best hope of a solution lay in the fact that the marriage had never been consummated. She was, rather naturally, almost wholly ignorant about the ways in which marriage could be dissolved, but she was pretty sure that somewhere she had heard mention of a thing called a decree of nullity. She would have to find out more about it before she broached the subject to Quentin. And she would have to set about finding a new home and planning a new life, for the one thing she could not endure was to go on living where she might meet him at any time and know that he no longer had any part in her life.

After which she stopped being brave and sensible and clear-headed, and cried herself to sleep like any other tired girl with a sore heart.

The final days in Merland House were busy ones. Having already made up her mind that she would never see the familiar rooms again, Pippa already felt herself a little detached from her surroundings. It was a depressing sensation and she buried it thankfully in zealous attention to packing. She looked a trifle heavy-eyed and subdued, but everyone except her husband ascribed this to a tiredness perfectly natural after so busy and brilliant a Season. Quentin, studying the tightly composed little face with thoughtful eyes, said that this time they would take two days over the journey so that she would not be so exhausted.

Preoccupied with her own miserable thoughts,

Pippa did not take her usual lively interest in the travelling arrangements. She bade Lady Cresswell a rather stilted farewell. It surprised and disappointed the recipient, who could not know that the girl was on the edge of tears, wondering if they would ever meet again and what her mother-in-law would think if she knew the true state of affairs.

Quentin had chosen to ride, so Pooley travelled with her mistress in the chaise, a second coach following with the amazing amount of baggage which had somehow accumulated during the weeks in Town. Pippa's groom, driving the phaeton, which Quentin had said she would certainly need in the country, brought up the rear. They lay overnight in Oxford, but when Quentin suggested a stroll through the ancient streets that beckoned invitation under the gentle moon, his wife excused herself, pleading fatigue. He did not press the matter, but said that she should breakfast in bed next day.

"We have only a short journey before us. No need for haste. We can spend a lazy morning exploring and still be home in time for dinner."

Pippa had no particular fancy for breakfast in bed, but she *did* wish to avoid her husband's society. At close quarters, and with only Pooley to serve as a barrier, his personality suddenly seemed overpowering. She knew that he would never do anything to hurt or frighten her, but in view of what she had to say to him she was understandably nervous. If his sense of obligation insisted, he was quite capable of bearing down her reasoned arguments. She would not know how to convince him that *her* way was the only honest and sensible one, and might even be coaxed—or coerced—she did not know which—into meek submission. The less she saw of him the better.

Despite her troubled mind she slept long and deeply, thanks to a sleeping draught which the obliging Pooley, obedient to her master's orders, had added to her bedtime tisane, and woke to find the sunshine streaming in at the casement and a smiling chamber-maid setting a well-laden tray on a chest that stood in the window. She was not particularly hungry but she drank the excellent coffee thirstily and ate a slice of bread and butter from a sense of duty. She felt oddly languid and relaxed, was thankful that there was no particular need for haste, but sprang anxiously to alarmed life when the chamber-maid, having born away the breakfast tray with a distinct air of reproach because the guest had rejected most of the proffered bounty, returned to enquire if she should help her ladyship to dress.

"But where is my own maid?" she demanded in startled tones.

The girl looked surprised. "Why, to be sure, milady, she went off in your coach. They set out early, I believe. Only his lordship said as how you was very tired and that he wanted you to have your sleep out."

Pippa's heart began to beat in hard, uneven thumps. Here was mystery and uncertainty. Here, just when she most needed Pooley's protective presence, Pooley had been removed. And without a word to her. Nothing had been said about an early departure. The last she had heard was that there was no call for haste.

She suffered the maid's ministrations abstractedly and sadly disappointed the poor girl by showing no interest at all in the arrangement of her hair, though she made more than adequate amends by the generosity of the vail that she bestowed. Then she left her to finish the packing, took her courage in both hands and went downstairs to look for her husband.

She found him in the coffee room, immersed in the Gazette—and was, ridiculously, surprised that he should appear his perfectly normal, casual self, because somehow, since they had left Town, he had grown into an unpredictable and ogre-ish kind of person. It was quite disconcerting to receive a pleasant good morning, a solicitous enquiry as to how she had slept, and the information that they were to finish the journey in the phaeton.

"I knew you wouldn't want to be cooped up in a stuffy chaise on such a fine morning," he told her confidently.

She comforted herself that there would be no

opportunity for private—and possibly awkward—conversation in a phaeton with a groom perched up behind, and went to put on her hat and pelisse. But when she came out into the sunny inn yard, it was a strange ostler who was holding the horses, and Quentin, having helped her up into her seat and tucked a rug over her knees, said cheerfully, "I thought we might dispense with Goulden this morning. If we *do* run into trouble it's a well frequented road—and I would be quite willing to entrust the horses to you while I went to summon assistance."

Since this handsome compliment won him no more than a mechanical smile of acknowledgement, he made no further attempts at conversation and devoted himself to his horses. It was obvious that Pippa had something on her mind, but no doubt she would make a clean breast of it when the moment was propitious. And he had done his share in arranging for that when he had made a clean sweep of the army of relatives and well-wishers who had hung around them ever since they married and had impeded his attempts at making that marriage a reality.

Despite her inner perturbation, Pippa's spirits rose insensibly to the swift, easy motion through the cool air, and her taut nerves began to relax. They stopped for coffee and a change of horses at a small wayside inn. It was a humble place, but the coffee, piping hot and drunk out of doors, was delicious. She wondered little about the horses, for this was not a posting house. But the animals that were presently brought out by the elderly ostler were no job horses. They were Quentin's own dapple greys and must have been brought over from Merland on his instructions. So this apparently casual interlude was not just an impulsive start, but a plan of action carefully thought out, perhaps several days previously.

It was puzzling, but she did not care to make enquiries which might lead to a difficult conversation, so she took her place in the phaeton without comment. Presently, however, she was betrayed into an exclamation of surprise. Quentin eased the horses to a walk and turned off the good pike road into a narrow twisting lane that was signposted for Daylesford.

"I thought we might as well go this way," he explained, steadying the greys who were taking exception to the proximity of the hedges. "I sent to Mrs. Waring advising her that we would probably do so. You will like to assure yourself that the place is in good order."

Pippa was not too sure about that. To be visiting the home where she had dreamed her shy dreams of a blissful future shared with the man beside her could only conjure up a painful comparison between past and present. But it would have to be endured.

Stubbs, his face one wide grin, came to take the horses, and informed their owner that it was a real pleasure to be handling decent cattle again. Mrs. Waring, curtseying primly, assured them that she had taken order for their coming and that a meal could be served as soon as they chose to eat.

"Excellent," pronounced his lordship. "For my part, I'm devilish sharp-set. How about you, my love?"

His love, who felt that food would choke her, said that she would like to take a turn about the garden first. To speak truth, the house, in its unnatural tidiness, seemed a hollow shell, full of dead dreams. It might be more bearable when Dickon and Cindy came back, but at the moment she wanted only to escape. Most certainly she must set about finding somewhere else to live.

Unfortunately the garden, too, was haunted. The berries had all been picked but she could have pointed out the very bush that she had been stripping when Quentin had sought her out to patch up a quarrel that had been of *her* making. Once again she recalled Uncle Philip's solemn advice about rooting out pride as one did weeds. But pride, alas, was all she had left to her.

Quite suddenly she could face no more. She turned to him abruptly and broke into impetuous speech. "Milord, I am glad to have this opportunity of speaking to you privately. It is one that I have been seeking these three days past."

216

He looked rather amused. "Have you, my dear? I am before you. *I* have been seeking that same opportunity ever since I returned from chasing after young Dickon."

"And now may spare yourself the pains, since I have learned the truth for myself."

Quentin was completely non-plussed. "The truth?" he repeated, on a note of enquiry.

"So I believe. It is true, is it not, that you did not really wish to marry me, and only offered for me because you felt that you had jeopardised my good name?"

Quentin was unprepared for this sudden attack. How, in any case, did one deal with a double-barrelled question which demanded two contradictory answers? He temporised.

"Honesty obliges me to admit that there is *some* truth in the charge," he began warily—and got no further.

Perhaps there had been a small lingering hope in Pippa's heart that he would deny her accusation. His tentative admission destroyed it—and with it the last shreds of her self-control. She turned on him fiercely.

"And I, of course, was allowed no say in a decision that affected my whole life. I daresay you even expect me to be grateful for your noble self-sacrifice. Well—I am *not* grateful. I never aspired to vast wealth and noble rank. I wanted a husband—a real one—and children born of our love. You offer me a hollow sham, with all the outward appearance of a happy

217

marriage and a complete denial of every normal womanly instinct. And I will have none of it. I am done with polite pretence; done with striving to make myself into the kind of wife suited to your top-lofty notions. From today I follow my own path. But for one thing at least I will render honest thanks. You have brought me home to my own place—and here you may leave me. Go back to Merland, my lord marquess, and divorce me. I no longer care for the stigma or the hideous publicity. Divorce me for denying you those rights that you never claimed —or indeed, desired. The bond between us cannot be dissolved too soon, for it has become a burden intolerable."

The first part of this outburst was, in part, lost on its audience, so stunned was he by the fury of the attack. But as the bitter words assailed his ears, it seemed to him that his wife was neither so determined nor so indifferent as she strove to appear. Hurt, miserable, angry; and with good cause. But not indifferent. And one other thing was made abundantly clear. If he allowed himself to become entangled in painstaking explanation and apology, he would be utterly lost. So explanation and apology must wait. There was only one thing to be done. Swiftly, deliberately, he took his wife in his arms and stifled the bitter words with kisses.

After the first startled moment she fought him with all her strength, but he only held her fast prisoned until she was breathless—and then kissed her again.

Presently he raised his head and said firmly, "And now, my small termagant, if you will listen to *me*, we will settle this business once and for all. No. Don't try to escape. I have you fast and mean to keep you so. I don't know which is the greater nonsense—your wild suggestion of divorce or your charge that I never loved you nor desired to claim my wife. Very well. So I *did* coax you into consenting to that hurried, furtive ceremony, because I had recklessly compromised you. And because I suspected—all too accurately, it would appear—that if the rumours that were circulating were to reach your ears, that fiery pride of yours would be up in arms and you would reject me out of hand. But I had been learning to love you ever since young Dickon thrust a miserable, soaking derelict upon your charity. And if you remember it was that same young man whose escapade summoned me from your side on our wedding night. Since when there has been no coming near you. Never did a man seek to win so elusive and straitly guarded a bride. While as for the succession of admirers that you have flaunted before me these past weeks, I was hard put to it not to try cooling their ardour by a little blood-letting. The only course open to me was to carry you off to some place where I could have you all to myself, without Mama or Emmy or Pooley or any other of your devoted bodyguard to come bursting in upon us. And that is precisely what I have done."

He stooped and kissed her again, more gently this time, as one who lingers over a treasured privilege. She made no resistance. In fact he thought there was a hint of response. He gathered her closer.

Pippa was remembering other kisses. Teasing—affectionate—dutiful, she had sometimes feared. Not like these. Her tired mind had scarcely grasped the meaning of his words though in a vague way they had brought comfort, but those firm, demanding kisses were using a language that she understood by instinct. She looked up at him, solemn-eyed, still hesitating to snatch at offered happiness.

"I think you are just being kind," she said slowly. "You must have realised by now that I'm not the right sort of wife for you. Thanks to your mother's artistic genius I scored something of a success—and I enjoyed it very much. But if I am to speak truth, I find I do not greatly care for a life that is one long succession of parties. They take up a great deal of time that I could have put to better use. You will think me very ungrateful and stupid, but I much prefer living in the country."

"*Exactly* the sort of wife for me," returned her husband, "since you express my own sentiments to a nicety. But you are quite mistaken about my 'kindness'. Just try keeping me at arms' length a little longer, and this you will discover, for if you will not come to me willingly I shall be obliged to enforce those rights of which you spoke with such eloquence. This endless shilly-shallying has been in part my fault, if never my choice. But the time has come to put an end to it."

Her heart was beating wildly in response to the determination in the voice, the steely strength in the arms that encircled her, but there was one memory that still stung. A sting that must be healed before she could make the surrender he demanded. It was not easy to put her last doubts into words, but she made a brave attempt.

"Then if, as you claim, you had—had learned to love me, why did you not come to me the night you came home after finding Dickon?"

He did not pretend to puzzlement. For the first time since they had left Town he looked a little less than confident, though he tried to carry it off with a high hand.

"That was quite your own fault," he assured her, though his shamefaced expression betrayed him. "Or perhaps partly Romsey's. Between the feast that *you* had chosen to set before me and *his* assiduous ministrations, I had been wined and dined until I was practically comatose. A warm fire and a certain degree of fatigue—understandable, you will agree—did the rest. I fell asleep."

Having at last made his confession he regarded her with an air half humorous, half penitent. Pippa remembered the long drawn out misery of that waiting; the growing sense of humiliation; the tears that had damped her pillow when, finally, she had put out her candle. He had fallen asleep! All her painful mortification for so simple a cause. For a moment she stared at him blankly, scarcely knowing herself which of the medley of emotions that filled her was paramount, certainly quite unable to find words to express them. And then the absurdity of the thing suddenly struck her, and the strain and uncertainty were swept away in an irrepressible fit of the giggles.

His lordship's doubtful expression vanished at that encouraging sign. He swept her into an embrace that left her neither the breath nor the inclination for further question or recrimination.

Presently he said contentedly, "None of our household knows that we are here. I said only that we meant to snatch a belated honeymoon and would let them know of our return in good time. Mrs. Waring will see to our meals and I will play lady's maid to the best of my ability, so that you will not miss the ministrations of Pooley."

She blushed a little for that, but only nuzzled her cheek trustfully against his shoulder. He hugged her fiercely, then with an impatient sigh, picked her up bodily and established her on the stump of an old apple tree, disposing himself on the sward at her feet, regardless of moss stains on his buckskins, and possessing himself of one slim hand which he proceeded to caress in a gentle, absent sort of way, tracing the lines on the soft palm with an intent forefinger and then filling it with kisses and folding the pliant fingers over them.

A splendid Tiger moth, glowing in black and gold, came hovering over them and settled on the soft ruffle that bordered Pippa's skirt.

"Look!" she whispered. "Isn't he beautiful?" And then, dreamily, "Do you remember the little green caterpillar that you picked out of my hair and put back in the bush? Wouldn't it be queer if *he* was that same caterpillar in this new and glorious guise?"

Quentin, who knew that this particular type of moth evolved from quite a different type of caterpillar, repressed a grin. But this was no time to be giving his wife lessons in natural history. There were much more interesting things to be done.

"It would indeed," he agreed, with perfect truth; and kissed her again.

# Let COVENTRY Give You
# A Little Old-Fashioned Romance